LET'S GET INVISIBLE!

Look for more Goosebumps books
by R.L. Stine:

Welcome to Dead House
Stay Out of the Basement
Monster Blood
Say Cheese and Die!
The Curse of the Mummy's Tomb

Goosebumps

LET'S GET INVISIBLE!

R. L. STINE

AN
APPLE
PAPERBACK

SCHOLASTIC INC.
New York Toronto London Auckland Sydney

ISBN 0-590-45370-X

12 11 10 9 8 7   3 4 5 6 7 8/9

Printed in the U.S.A.   40

First Scholastic printing, March 1993

1

I went invisible for the first time on my twelfth birthday.

It was all Whitey's fault, in a way. Whitey is my dog. He's just a mutt, part terrier, part everything else. He's all black, so of course we named him Whitey.

If Whitey hadn't been sniffing around in the attic . . .

Well, maybe I'd better back up a bit and start at the beginning.

My birthday was on a rainy Saturday. It was a few minutes before kids would start arriving for my birthday party, so I was getting ready.

Getting ready means brushing my hair.

My brother is always on my case about my hair. He gives me a hard time because I spend so much time in front of the mirror brushing it and checking it out.

The thing is, I just happen to have great hair. It's very thick and sort of a golden brown, and just a little bit wavy. My hair is my best feature, so I like to make sure it looks okay.

Also, I have very big ears. They stick out a lot. So I have to keep making sure that my hair covers my ears. It's important.

"Max, it's messed up in back," my brother, Lefty, said, standing behind me as I studied my hair in the front hall mirror.

His name is really Noah, but I call him Lefty because he's the only left-handed person in our family. Lefty was tossing a softball up and catching it in his left hand. He knew he wasn't supposed to toss that softball around in the house, but he always did it anyway.

Lefty is two years younger than me. He's not a bad guy, but he has too much energy. He always has to be tossing a ball around, drumming his hands on the table, hitting something, running around, falling down, leaping into things, wrestling with me. You get the idea. Dad says that Lefty has ants in his pants. It's a dumb expression, but it sort of describes my brother.

I turned and twisted my neck to see the back of my hair. "It is *not* messed up, liar," I said.

"Think fast!" Lefty shouted, and he tosssed the softball at me.

I made a grab for it and missed. It hit the wall just below the mirror with a loud *thud*. Lefty and I held our breath, waiting to see if Mom heard the sound. But she didn't. I think she was in the

2

kitchen doing something to the birthday cake.

"That was dumb," I whispered to Lefty. "You almost broke the mirror."

"*You're* dumb," he said. Typical.

"Why don't you learn to throw right-handed? Then maybe I could catch it sometimes," I told him. I liked to tease him about being left-handed because he really hated it.

"You stink," he said, picking up the softball.

I was used to it. He said it a hundred times a day. I guess he thought it was clever or something.

He's a good kid for a ten-year-old, but he doesn't have much of a vocabulary.

"Your ears are sticking out," he said.

I knew he was lying. I started to answer him, but the doorbell rang.

He and I raced down the narrow hallway to the front door. "Hey, it's *my* party!" I told him.

But Lefty got to the door first and pulled it open.

My best friend, Zack, pulled open the screen door and hurried into the house. It was starting to rain pretty hard, and he was already soaked.

He handed me a present, wrapped in silver paper, raindrops dripping off it. "It's a bunch of comic books," he said. "I already read 'em. The *X-Force* graphic novel is kind of cool."

"Thanks," I said. "They don't look too wet."

Lefty grabbed the present from my hand and

ran into the living room with it. "Don't open it!"
I shouted. He said he was just starting a pile.

Zack took off his Red Sox cap, and I got a look
at his new haircut. "Wow! You look . . . different,"
I said, studying his new look. His black hair was
buzzed real short on the left side. The rest of it
was long, brushed straight to the right.

"Did you invite girls?" he asked me, "or is it
just boys?"

"Some girls are coming," I told him. "Erin and
April. Maybe my cousin Debra." I knew he liked
Debra.

He nodded thoughtfully. Zack has a real serious
face. He has these little blue eyes that always look
far away, like he's thinking hard about something.
Like he's real deep.

He's sort of an intense guy. Not nervous. Just
keyed up. And very competitive. He has to win
at everything. If he comes in second place, he gets
really upset and kicks the furniture. You know
the kind.

"What are we going to do?" Zack asked, shaking
the water off his Red Sox cap.

I shrugged. "We were supposed to be in the
back yard. Dad put the volleyball net up this
morning. But that was before it started to rain.
I rented some movies. Maybe we'll watch them."

The doorbell rang. Lefty appeared again from
out of nowhere, pushed Zack and me out of the

way, and made a dive for the door. "Oh, it's you," I heard him say.

"Thanks for the welcome." I recognized Erin's squeaky voice. Some kids call Erin "Mouse" because of that voice, and because she's tiny like a mouse. She has short, straight blonde hair, and I think she's cute, but of course I'd never tell anyone that.

"Can we come in?" I recognized April's voice next. April is the other girl in our group. She has curly black hair and dark, sad eyes. I always thought she was really sad, but then I figured out that she's just shy.

"The party's tomorrow," I heard Lefty tell them.

"Huh?" Both girls uttered cries of surprise.

"No, it isn't," I shouted. I stepped into the doorway and shoved Lefty out of the way. I pushed open the screen door so Erin and April could come in. "You know Lefty's little jokes," I said, squeezing my brother against the wall.

"Lefty *is* a little joke," Erin said.

"You're stupid," Lefty told her. I pressed him into the wall a little harder, leaning against him with all my weight. But he ducked down and scooted away.

"Happy Birthday," April said, shaking the rain from her curly hair. She handed me a present, wrapped in Christmas wrapping paper. "It's the only paper we had," she explained, seeing me staring at it.

"Merry Christmas to you, too," I joked. The present felt like a CD.

"I forgot your present," Erin said.

"What is it?" I asked, following the girls into the living room.

"I don't know. I haven't bought it yet."

Lefty grabbed April's present out of my hand and ran to put it on top of Zack's present in the corner behind the couch.

Erin plopped down on the white leather ottoman in front of the armchair. April stood at the window, staring out at the rain.

"We were going to barbecue hot dogs," I said.

"They'd be pretty soggy today," April replied.

Lefty stood behind the couch, tossing his softball up and catching it one-handed.

"You're going to break that lamp," I warned him.

He ignored me, of course.

"Who else is coming?" Erin asked.

Before I could answer, the doorbell rang again. Lefty and I raced to the door. He tripped over his own sneakers and went skidding down the hall on his stomach. So typical.

By two-thirty everyone had arrived, fifteen kids in all, and the party got started. Well, it didn't really get started because we couldn't decide what to do. I wanted to watch the *Terminator* movie

I'd rented. But the girls wanted to play Twister. "It's *my* birthday!" I insisted.

We compromised. We played Twister. Then we watched some of the *Terminator* video until it was time to eat.

It was a pretty good party. I think everyone had an okay time. Even April seemed to be having fun. She was usually really quiet and nervous-looking at parties.

Lefty spilled his Coke and ate his slice of chocolate birthday cake with his hands because he thought it was funny. But he was the only animal in the group.

I told him the only reason he was invited was because he was in the family and there was nowhere else we could stash him. He replied by opening his mouth up real wide so everyone could see his chewed-up chocolate cake inside.

After I opened presents, I put the *Terminator* movie back on. But everyone started to leave. I guess it was about five o'clock. It looked much later. It was dark as night out, still storming.

My parents were in the kitchen cleaning up. Erin and April were the only ones left. Erin's mother was supposed to pick them up. She called and said she'd be a little late.

Whitey was standing at the living room window, barking his head off. I looked outside. I didn't see anyone there. I grabbed him with both hands and wrestled him away from the window.

7

"Let's go up to my room," I suggested when I finally got the dumb dog quiet. "I got a new Super Nintendo game I want to try."

Erin and April gladly followed me upstairs. They didn't like the *Terminator* movie, for some reason.

The upstairs hallway was pitch black. I clicked the light switch, but the overhead light didn't come on. "The bulb must be burned out," I said.

My room was at the end of the hall. We made our way slowly through the darkness.

"It's kind of spooky up here," April said quietly.

And just as she said it, the linen closet door swung open and, with a deafening howl, a dark figure leapt out at us.

2

As the girls cried out in horror, the howling creature grabbed me around the waist and wrestled me to the floor.

"Lefty — *let go!*" I screamed angrily. "You're not funny!"

He was laughing like a lunatic. He thought he was a riot. "Gotcha!" he cried. "I gotcha good!"

"We weren't scared," Erin insisted. "We knew it was you."

"Then why'd you scream?" Lefty asked.

Erin didn't have an answer.

I shoved him off me and climbed to my feet. "That was dumb, Lefty."

"How long were you waiting in the linen closet?" April asked.

"A long time," Lefty told her. He started to get up, but Whitey ran up to him and began furiously licking his face. It tickled so much, Lefty fell onto his back, laughing.

"You scared Whitey, too," I said.

9

"No, I didn't. Whitey's smarter than you guys."
Lefty pushed Whitey away.

Whitey began sniffing at the door across the hall.

"Where does that door lead, Max?" Erin asked.

"To the attic," I told her.

"You have an attic?" Erin cried. Like it was some kind of big deal. "What's up there? I *love* attics!"

"Huh?" I squinted at her in the dark. Sometimes girls are really weird. I mean, how could anyone *love* attics?

"Just a lot of old junk my grandparents left," I told her. "This house used to be theirs. Mom and Dad stored a lot of their stuff in the attic. We hardly ever go up there."

"Can we go up and take a look?" Erin asked.

"I guess," I said. "I don't think it's too big a thrill or anything."

"I love old junk," Erin said.

"But it's so dark. . . ." April said softly. I think she was a little scared.

I opened the door and reached for the light switch just inside. A ceiling light clicked on in the attic. It cast a pale yellow light down at us as we stared up the steep wooden stairs.

"See? There's light up there," I told April. I started up the stairs. They creaked under my sneakers. My shadow was really long. "You coming?"

10

"Erin's mom will be here any minute," April said.

"We'll just go up for a second," Erin said. She gave April a gentle push. "Come on."

Whitey trotted past us as we climbed the stairs, his tail wagging excitedly, his toenails clicking loudly on the wooden steps. About halfway up, the air grew hot and dry.

I stopped on the top step and looked around. The attic stretched on both sides. It was one long room, filled with old furniture, cardboard cartons, old clothes, fishing rods, stacks of yellowed magazines — all kinds of junk.

"Ooh, it smells so musty," Erin said, moving past me and taking a few steps into the vast space. She took a deep breath. "I love that smell!"

"You're definitely weird," I told her.

Rain drummed loudly against the roof. The sound echoed through the low room, a steady roar. It sounded as if we were inside a waterfall.

All four of us began walking around, exploring. Lefty kept tossing his softball up against the ceiling rafters, then catching it as it came down. I noticed that April stayed close to Erin. Whitey was sniffing furiously along the wall.

"Think there are mice up here?" Lefty asked, a devilish grin crossing his face. I saw April's eyes go wide. "Big fat mice who like to climb up girls' legs?" Lefty teased.

My kid brother has a great sense of humor.

11

"Could we go now?" April asked impatiently. She started back toward the stairway.

"Look at these old magazines," Erin exclaimed, ignoring her. She picked one up and started flipping through it. "Check this out. The clothes these models are wearing are a riot!"

"Hey — what's Whitey doing?" Lefty asked suddenly.

I followed his gaze to the far wall. Behind a tall stack of cartons, I could see Whitey's tail wagging. And I could hear him scratching furiously at something.

"Whitey — come!" I commanded.

Of course he ignored me. He began scratching harder.

"Whitey, what are you scratching at?"

"Probably pulling a mouse apart," Lefty suggested.

"I'm outta here!" April exclaimed.

"Whitey?" I called. Stepping around an old dining room table, I made my way across the cluttered attic. I quickly saw that he was scratching at the bottom of a door.

"Hey, look," I called to the others. "Whitey found a hidden door."

"Cool!" Erin cried, hurrying over. Lefty and April were right behind.

"I didn't know this was up here," I said.

"We've got to check it out," Erin urged. "Let's see what's on the other side."

And that's when the trouble all began.

You can understand why I say it was all Whitey's fault, right? If that dumb dog hadn't started sniffing and scratching there, we might never have found the hidden attic room.

And we never would have discovered the exciting — and frightening — secret behind that wooden door.

3

"Whitey!" I knelt down and pulled the dog away from the door. "What's your problem, doggie?"

As soon as I moved him aside, Whitey lost all interest in the door. He trotted off and started sniffing another corner. Talk about your short attention span. But I guess that's the difference between dogs and people.

The rain continued to pound down, a steady roar just above our heads. I could hear the wind whistling around the corner of the house. It was a real spring storm.

The door had a rusted latch about halfway up. It slid off easily, and the warped wooden door started to swing open before I even pulled at it.

The door hinges squeaked as I pulled the door toward me, revealing solid darkness on the other side.

Before I had gotten the door open halfway, Lefty scooted under me and darted into the dark room.

"*A dead body!*" he shrieked.

"Noooo!" April and Erin both cried out with squeals of terror.

But I knew Lefty's dumb sense of humor. "Nice try, Lefty," I said, and followed him through the doorway.

Of course he was just goofing.

I found myself in a small, windowless room. The only light came from the pale yellow ceiling light behind us in the center of the attic.

"Push the door all the way open so the light can get in," I instructed Erin. "I can't see a thing in here."

Erin pushed open the door and slid a carton over to hold it in place. Then she and April crept in to join Lefty and me.

"It's too big to be a closet," Erin said, her voice sounding even squeakier than usual. "So what is it?"

"Just a room, I guess," I said, still waiting for my eyes to adjust to the dim light.

I took another step into the room. And as I did, a dark figure stepped toward me.

I screamed and jumped back.

The other person jumped back, too.

"It's a mirror, dork!" Lefty said, and started to laugh.

Instantly, all four of us were laughing. Nervous, high-pitched laughter.

It *was* a mirror in front of us. In the pale yellow

15

light filtering into the small, square room, I could see it clearly now.

It was a big, rectangular mirror, about two feet taller than me, with a dark wood frame. It rested on a wooden base.

I moved closer to it and my reflection moved once again to greet me. To my surprise, the reflection was clear. No dust on the glass, despite the fact that no one had been in here in ages.

I stepped in front of it and started to check out my hair.

I mean, that's what mirrors are for, right?

"Who would put a mirror in a room all by itself?" Erin asked. I could see her dark reflection in the mirror, a few feet behind me.

"Maybe it's a valuable piece of furniture or something," I said, reaching into my jeans pocket for my comb. "You know. An antique."

"Did your parents put it up here?" Erin asked.

"I don't know," I replied. "Maybe it belonged to my grandparents. I just don't know." I ran the comb through my hair a few times.

"Can we go now? This isn't too thrilling," April said. She was still lingering reluctantly in the doorway.

"Maybe it was a carnival mirror," Lefty said, pushing me out of the way and making faces into the mirror, bringing his face just inches from the glass. "You know. One of those fun house mirrors

16

that makes your body look like it's shaped like an egg."

"You're already shaped like an egg," I joked, pushing him aside. "At least, your head is."

"You're a *rotten* egg," he snapped back. "You stink."

I peered into the mirror. I looked perfectly normal, not distorted at all. "Hey, April, come in," I urged. "You're blocking most of the light."

"Can't we just leave?" she asked, whining. Reluctantly, she moved from the doorway, taking a few small steps into the room. "Who cares about an old mirror, anyway?"

"Hey, look," I said, pointing. I had spotted a light attached to the top of the mirror. It was oval-shaped, made of brass or some other kind of metal. The bulb was long and narrow, almost like a fluorescent bulb, only shorter.

I gazed up at it, trying to figure it out in the dim light. "How do you turn it on, I wonder."

"There's a chain," Erin said, coming up beside me.

Sure enough, a slender chain descended from the right side of the lamp, hanging down about a foot from the top of the mirror.

"Wonder if it works," I said.

"The bulb's probably dead," Lefty remarked. Good old Lefty. Always an optimist.

"Only one way to find out," I said. Standing on

tiptoes, I stretched my hand up to the chain.

"Be careful," April warned.

"Huh? It's just a light," I told her.

Famous last words.

I reached up. Missed. Tried again. I grabbed the chain on the second try and pulled.

The light came on with a startlingly bright flash. Then it dimmed down to normal light. Very white light that reflected brightly in the mirror.

"Hey — that's better!" I exclaimed. "It lights up the whole room. Pretty bright, huh?"

No one said anything.

"I *said*, pretty bright, huh?"

Still silence from my companions.

I turned around and was surprised to find looks of horror on all three faces.

"Max?" Lefty cried, staring hard at me, his eyes practically popping out of his head.

"Max — where are you?" Erin cried. She turned to April. "Where'd he go?"

"I'm right here," I told them. "I haven't moved."

"*But we can't see you!*" April cried.

4

All three of them were staring in my direction with their eyes bulging and looks of horror still on their faces. But I could tell they were goofing.

"Give me a break, guys," I said. "I'm not as stupid as I look. No way I'm falling for your dumb joke."

"But, Max — " Lefty insisted. "We're *serious!*"

"We can't see you!" Erin repeated.

Dumb, dumb, dumb.

Suddenly, the light started to hurt my eyes. It seemed to grow brighter. It was shining right in my face.

Shielding my eyes with one hand, I reached up with the other hand and pulled the chain.

The light went out, but the white glare stayed with me. I tried to blink it away, but I still saw large bright spots before my eyes.

"Hey — you're back!" Lefty cried. He stepped up and grabbed my arm and squeezed it, as if he were testing it, making sure I was real or something.

"What's your problem?" I snapped. I was starting to get angry. "I didn't fall for your dumb joke, Lefty. So why keep it up?"

To my surprise, Lefty didn't back away. He held onto my arm as if he were afraid to let go.

"We weren't joking, Max," Erin insisted in a low voice. "We really couldn't see you."

"It must have been the light in the mirror," April said. She was pressed against the wall next to the doorway. "It was so bright. I think it was just an optical illusion or something."

"It *wasn't* an optical illusion," Erin told her. "I was standing right next to Max. And I couldn't see him."

"He was invisible," Lefty added solemnly.

I laughed. "You guys are trying to scare me," I said. "And you're doing a pretty good job of it!"

"You scared *us!*" Lefty exclaimed. He let go of my arm and stepped up to the mirror.

I followed his gaze. "There I am," I said, pointing to my reflection. A strand of hair was poking up in back of my head. I carefully slicked it down.

"Let's get out of here," April pleaded.

Lefty started to toss his softball up, studying himself in the mirror.

Erin made her way around to the back of the mirror. "It's too dark back here. I can't see anything," she said.

She stepped around to the front and stared up at the oval-shaped lamp on top. "You disappeared as soon as you pulled the chain on that lamp."

"You're really serious!" I said. For the first time I began to believe they weren't joking.

"You were invisible, Max," Erin said. "Poof. You were gone."

"She's right," Lefty agreed, tossing the softball up and catching it, admiring his form in the mirror.

"It was just an optical illusion," April insisted. "Why are you guys making such a big deal about it?"

"It *wasn't*!" Erin insisted.

"He clicked on the light. Then he disappeared in a flash," Lefty said. He dropped the softball. It bounced loudly on the hardwood floor, then rolled behind the mirror.

He hesitated for a few seconds. Then he went after it, diving for the ball in the darkness. A few seconds later, he came running back.

"You really were invisible, Max," he said.

"Really," Erin added, staring hard at me.

"Prove it," I told them.

"Let's *go*!" April pleaded. She had moved to the doorway and was standing half in, half out of the room.

"What do you mean *prove it*?" Erin asked, talking to my dark reflection in the mirror.

"Show me," I said.

"You mean do what you did?" Erin asked, turning to talk to the real me.

"Yeah," I said. "You go invisible, too. Just like I did."

Erin and Lefty stared at me. Lefty's mouth dropped open.

"This is dumb," April called from behind us.

"I'll do it," Lefty said. He stepped up to the mirror.

I pulled him back by the shoulders. "Not you," I said. "You're too young."

He tried to pull out of my grasp, but I held onto him. "How about you, Erin?" I urged, wrapping my arms around Lefty's waist to keep him back from the mirror.

She shrugged. "Okay. I'll try, I guess."

Lefty stopped struggling to get away. I loosened my grip a little.

We watched Erin step up in front of the mirror. Her reflection stared back at her, dark and shadowy.

She stood on tiptoes, reached up, and grabbed the lamp chain. She glanced over at me and smiled. "Here goes," she said.

5

The chain slipped from Erin's hand.

She reached up and grabbed it again.

She was just about to tug at it when a woman's voice interrupted from downstairs. "Erin! Are you up there? April?"

I recognized the voice. Erin's mom.

"Yeah. We're up here," Erin shouted. She let go of the chain.

"Hurry down. We're late!" her mom called. "What are you doing up in the attic, anyway?"

"Nothing," Erin called down. She turned to me and shrugged.

"Good. I'm *outta* here!" April exclaimed, and hurried to the stairway.

We all followed her down, clumping noisily down the creaking wooden stairs.

"What were you doing up there?" my mom asked when we were all in the living room. "It's so dusty in that attic. It's a wonder you're not filthy."

"We were just hanging out," I told her.

"We were playing with an old mirror," Lefty said. "It was kind of neat."

"Playing with a mirror?" Erin's mom flashed my mom a bewildered glance.

"See you guys," Erin said, pulling her mom to the door. "Great party, Max."

"Yeah. Thanks," April added.

They headed out the front door. The rain had finally stopped. I stood at the screen door and watched them step around the puddles on the walk as they made their way to the car.

When I turned back into the living room, Lefty was tossing the softball up to the ceiling, trying to catch it behind his back. He missed. The ball bounced up from the floor onto an end table, where it knocked over a large vase of tulips.

What a crash!

The vase shattered. Tulips went flying. All the water poured down onto the carpet.

Mom tossed up her hands and said something silently up to the sky, the way she always does when she's very pushed out of shape about something.

Then she really got on Lefty's case. She started screaming: "How many times do I have to tell you not to throw that ball in the house?" Stuff like that. She kept it up for quite a while.

Lefty shrank into a corner and tried to make himself tinier and tinier. He kept saying he was sorry, but Mom was yelling so loud, I don't think she heard him.

I bet Lefty wanted to be invisible right at that moment.

But he had to stand and take his punishment.

Then he and I helped clean up the mess.

A few minutes later, I saw him tossing the softball up in the living room again.

That's the thing about Lefty. He never learns.

I didn't think about the mirror again for a couple of days. I got busy with school and other stuff. Rehearsing for the spring concert. I'm only in the chorus, but I still have to go to every rehearsal.

I saw Erin and April in school a lot. But neither of them mentioned the mirror. I guess maybe it slipped their minds, too. Or maybe we all just shut it out of our minds.

It was kind of scary, if you stopped to think about it.

I mean, *if* you believed what they said happened.

Then that Wednesday night I couldn't get to sleep. I was lying there, staring up at the ceiling, watching the shadows sway back and forth.

I tried counting sheep. I tried shutting my eyes real tight and counting backwards from one thousand.

But I was really keyed up, for some reason. Not at all sleepy.

Suddenly I found myself thinking about the mirror up in the attic.

What was it doing up there? I asked myself. Why was it closed up in that hidden room with the door carefully latched?

Who did it belong to? My grandparents? If so, why would they hide it in that tiny room?

I wondered if Mom and Dad even knew it was up there.

I started thinking about what had happened on Saturday after my birthday party. I pictured myself standing in front of the mirror. Combing my hair. Then reaching for the chain. Pulling it. The flash of bright light as the lamp went on. And then . . .

Did I see my reflection in the mirror after the light went on?

I couldn't remember.

Did I see myself at all? My hands? My feet?

I couldn't remember.

"It was a joke," I said aloud, lying in my bed, kicking the covers off me.

It had to be a joke.

Lefty was always playing dumb jokes on me, trying to make me look bad. My brother was a joker. He'd always been a joker. He was never serious. Never.

So what made me think he was serious now?

Because Erin and April had agreed with him?

Before I realized it, I had climbed out of bed.

Only one way to find out if they were serious or not, I told myself. I searched in the darkness for my bedroom slippers. I buttoned my pajama shirt which had come undone from all my tossing and turning.

Then, as silent as I could be, I crept out into the hallway.

The house was dark except for the tiny night-light down by the floor just outside Lefty's bedroom. Lefty was the only one in the family who ever got up in the middle of the night. He insisted on having a night-light in his room and one in the hall, even though I made fun of him about it as often as I could.

Now I was grateful for the light as I made my way on tiptoe to the attic stairs. Even though I was being so careful, the floorboards squeaked under my feet. It's just impossible not to make noise in an old house like this.

I stopped and held my breath, listening hard, listening for any sign that I had been heard.

Silence.

Taking a deep breath, I opened the attic door, fumbled around till I found the light switch, and clicked on the attic light. Then I made my way slowly up the steep stairs, leaning all my weight on the banister, trying my hardest not to make the stairs creak.

It seemed to take forever to get all the way up. Finally, I stopped at the top step and gazed around, letting my eyes adjust to the yellow glare of the ceiling light.

The attic was hot and stuffy. The air was so dry, it made my nose burn. I had a sudden urge to turn around and go back.

But then my eyes stopped at the doorway to the small, hidden room. In our hurry to leave, we had left the door wide open.

Staring at the darkness beyond the open doorway, I stepped onto the landing and made my way quickly across the cluttered floor. The floorboards creaked and groaned beneath me, but I barely heard them.

I was drawn to the open doorway, drawn to the mysterious room as if being pulled by a powerful magnet.

I had to see the tall mirror again. I had to examine it, study it closely.

I had to know the truth about it.

I stepped into the small room without hesitating and walked up to the mirror.

I paused for a moment and studied my shadowy reflection in the glass. My hair was totally messed up, but I didn't care.

I stared at myself, stared into my eyes. Then I took a step back to get a different view.

The mirror reflected my entire body from head to foot. There wasn't anything special about the reflection. It wasn't distorted or weird in any way.

The fact that it was such a normal reflection

helped to calm me. I hadn't realized it, but my heart was fluttering like a nervous butterfly. My hands and feet were cold as ice.

"Chill out, Max," I whispered to myself, watching myself whisper in the dark mirror.

I did a funny little dance for my own benefit, waving my hands above my head and shaking my whole body.

"Nothing special about this mirror," I said aloud.

I reached out and touched it. The glass felt cool despite the warmth of the room. I ran my hand along the glass until I reached the frame. Then I let my hand wander up and down the wood frame. It also felt smooth and cool.

It's just a mirror, I thought, finally feeling more relaxed. Just an old mirror that someone stored up here long ago and forgot about.

Still holding onto the frame, I walked around to the back. It was too dark to see clearly, but it didn't seem too interesting back here.

Well, I might as well turn on the light at the top, I thought.

I returned to the front of the mirror. Standing just inches back from it, I began to reach up for the lamp chain when something caught my eye.

"Oh!"

I cried out as I saw two eyes, down low in the mirror. Two eyes staring out at me.

6

My breath caught in my throat. I peered down into the dark reflection.

The two eyes peered up at me. Dark and evil eyes.

Uttering a cry of panic, I turned away from the mirror.

"Lefty!" I cried. My voice came out shrill and tight, as if someone were squeezing my throat.

He grinned at me from just inside the doorway.

I realized that it had been Lefty's eyes reflected in the mirror.

I ran over to him and grabbed him by the shoulders. "You scared me to death!" I half-screamed, half-whispered.

His grin grew wider. "You're stupid," he said.

I wanted to strangle him. He thought it was a riot.

"Why'd you sneak up behind me?" I demanded, giving him a shove back against the wall.

He shrugged.

"Well, what are you doing up here, anyway?"
I sputtered.

I could still see those dark eyes staring out at me in the mirror. So creepy!

"I heard you," he explained, leaning back against the wall, still grinning. "I was awake. I heard you walk past my room. So I followed you."

"Well, you shouldn't be up here," I snapped.

"Neither should you," he snapped back.

"Go back downstairs and go to bed," I said. My voice was finally returning to normal. I tried to sound as if I meant business.

But Lefty didn't move. "Make me," he said. Another classic argument-winner.

"I mean it," I insisted. "Go back to bed."

"Make me," he repeated nastily. "I'll tell Mom and Dad you're up here," he added.

I hate being threatened. And he knows it. That's why he threatens me every hour of the day.

Sometimes I just wish I could pound him.

But we live in a nonviolent family.

That's what Mom and Dad say every time Lefty and I get in a fight. "Break it up, you two. We live in a nonviolent family."

Sometimes nonviolence can be real frustrating. Know what I mean?

This was one of those times. But I could see that I wasn't going to get rid of Lefty so easily. He was determined to stay up in the attic with me and see what I was doing with the mirror.

My heart had finally slowed down to normal. I was starting to feel calmer. So I decided to stop fighting with him and let him stay. I turned back to the mirror.

Luckily, there wasn't *another* pair of eyes in there staring out at me!

"What are you doing?" Lefty demanded, stepping up behind me, his arms still crossed over his chest.

"Just checking out the mirror," I told him.

"You going to go invisible again?" he asked. He was standing right behind me, and his breath smelled sour, like lemons.

I turned and shoved him back a few steps. "Get out of my face," I said. "Your breath stinks."

That started another stupid argument, of course.

I was sorry I'd ever come up here. I should have stayed in bed, I realized.

Finally, I persuaded him to stand a foot away from me. A major victory.

Yawning, I turned back to the mirror. I was starting to feel sleepy. Maybe it was because of the heat of the attic. Maybe it was because I was tired of arguing with my dopey brother. Or maybe it was because it was really late at night, and I was tired.

"I'm going to turn on the light," I told him, reaching for the chain. "Tell me if I go invisible again."

"No." He shoved his way right next to me again. "I want to try it, too."

"No way," I insisted, shoving back.

"Yes *way*." He pushed me hard.

I pushed back. Then I had a better idea. "How about if we *both* stand in front of the mirror, and I pull the light chain?"

"Okay. Go ahead." Standing an inch in front of it, practically nose to nose with his reflection, Lefty stiffened until he was standing at attention.

He looked ridiculous, especially in those awful green pajamas.

I stepped up beside him. "Here goes nothing," I said.

I stretched my hand up, grabbed the light chain, and pulled.

7

The light on top of the mirror flashed.

"Ow!" I cried out. The light was so bright, it hurt my eyes.

Then it quickly dimmed, and my eyes started to adjust.

I turned to Lefty and started to say something. I don't remember what it was. It completely flew out of my mind when I realized that Lefty was gone.

"L-Lefty?" I stammered.

"I'm right here," he replied. His voice sounded nearby, but I couldn't see him. "Max — where are *you*?"

"You can't see me?" I cried.

"No," Lefty said. "No, I can't."

I could smell his sour breath, so I knew he was there. But he was invisible. Gone. Out of sight.

So they *weren't* putting me on! Erin, April, and Lefty had been telling the truth on Saturday after my birthday party. I really had gone invisible.

And now I was invisible again, along with my brother.

"Hey, Max," his voice sounded tiny, shaky. "This is weird."

"Yeah. It's weird, okay," I agreed. "You really can't see me, Lefty?"

"No. And I can't see myself," he said.

The mirror. I had forgotten to check out the mirror.

Did I have a reflection?

I turned and stared into the mirror. The light was pouring down from the top of the frame, casting a bright glare over the glass.

Squinting into the glare, I saw . . . *nothing.*

No me.

No Lefty.

Just the reflection of the wall behind us and the open doorway leading to the rest of the attic.

"We — we don't have reflections," I said.

"It's kinda cool," Lefty remarked. He grabbed my arm. I jumped in surprise.

"Hey!" I cried.

It felt creepy to be grabbed by an invisible person.

I grabbed him back. I tickled his ribs. He started to laugh.

"We still have our bodies," I said. "We just can't see them."

He tried to tickle me, but I danced away from him.

"Hey, Max, where'd you go?" he called, sounding frightened again.

"Try and find me," I teased, backing toward the wall.

"I — I can't," he said shakily. "Come back over here, okay?"

"No way," I said. "I don't want to be tickled."

"I won't," Lefty swore. "I promise."

I stepped back in front of the mirror.

"Are you here?" Lefty asked timidly.

"Yeah. I'm right beside you. I can smell your bad breath," I told him.

And he started to tickle me again. The little liar.

We wrestled around for a bit. It was just so strange wrestling with someone you couldn't see.

Finally, I pushed him away. "I wonder if we could go downstairs and still be invisible," I said. "I wonder if we could leave the house like this."

"And go spy on people?" Lefty suggested.

"Yeah," I said. I yawned. I was starting to feel a little strange. "We could go spy on girls and stuff."

"Cool," Lefty replied.

"Remember that old movie Mom and Dad were watching on TV?" I asked him. "About the ghosts who kept appearing and disappearing all the time? They had a lot of fun scaring people. You know, playing jokes on them, driving them crazy."

"But we're not ghosts," Lefty replied in a trembling voice. I think the idea kind of frightened him.

It frightened me, too!

"Could we go back to normal now?" Lefty asked. "I don't feel right."

"Me, either," I told him. I was feeling very light. Kind of fluttery. Just . . . weird.

"How can we get back right again?" he asked.

"Well, the last time, I just pulled the chain. I clicked the light off, and I was back. That's all it took."

"Well, do it," Lefty urged impatiently. "Right now. Okay?"

"Yeah. Okay." I started to feel kind of dizzy. Kind of light. As if I could float away or something.

"Hurry," Lefty said. I could hear him breathing hard.

I reached up and grabbed the light chain. "No problem," I told him. "We'll be back in a second."

I pulled the chain.

The light went out.

But Lefty and I didn't return.

"Max — I can't see you!" Lefty whined.

"I know," I replied quietly. I felt so frightened. I had chills running down my back, chills that wouldn't stop. "I can't see you, either."

"What happened?" Lefty cried. I could feel him tug at my invisible arm.

"I — I don't know," I stammered. "It worked before. I clicked off the light and I was back."

I gazed into the mirror. No reflection. Nothing. No me. No Lefty.

I stood there, staring at the spot where our reflections should be, frozen with fear. I was glad Lefty couldn't see me because I wouldn't want him to see how frightened I looked.

"Try it again, Max," he whined. "Please. Hurry!"

"Okay," I said. "Just try to stay calm, okay?"

"Stay calm? How?" Lefty wailed. "What if we *never* get back? What if *no one* can ever see us again?"

I suddenly felt so sick. My stomach just sort of heaved.

Get a grip, I told myself. You've *got* to keep it together, Max. For Lefty's sake.

I stretched up for the light chain, but it seemed to be out of my reach.

I tried again. Missed.

And then suddenly, I was back. And so was Lefty.

We could see each other. And we could see our reflections in the mirror.

"We're *back!*" We both shouted it in unison.

And then we both fell on the floor, laughing. We were so relieved. So happy.

"Ssshh!" I grabbed Lefty and shoved my hand over his mouth. I just remembered it was the middle of the night. "If Mom and Dad catch us up here, they'll kill us," I warned, whispering.

"Why did it take so long for us to come back?" Lefty asked, turning serious, gazing at his reflection.

I shrugged. "Beats me." I thought about it. "Maybe if you stay invisible longer, it takes longer for you to get back," I suggested.

"Huh? What do you mean?"

"The first time I went invisible," I told him, "it was only for a few seconds. And I came back instantly, as soon as I clicked off the light. But tonight — "

"We stayed invisible a lot longer. So it took

longer to come back. I get it," Lefty said.

"You're not as dumb as you look," I said, yawning.

"*You* are!" he snapped back.

Feeling totally exhausted, I started to lead the way out of the tiny room, motioning for Lefty to follow me. But he hesitated, glancing back at his reflection in the mirror.

"We have to tell Mom and Dad about the mirror," he whispered thoughtfully.

"No way!" I told him. "No way we're telling them. If we tell them about it, they'll take it away. They won't let us use it."

He stared at me thoughtfully. "I'm not sure I *want* to use it," he said softly.

"Well, I do," I said, turning at the doorway to look back at it. "I want to use it just one more time."

"What for?" Lefty asked, yawning.

"To scare Zack," I said, grinning.

Zack couldn't come over until Saturday. As soon as he arrived, I wanted to take him up to the attic and give him a demonstration of the mirror's powers.

Mainly, I wanted to scare the life out of him!

But Mom insisted that we sit down for lunch first. Canned chicken noodle soup and peanut butter-and-jelly sandwiches.

I gulped my soup as fast as I could, not both-

40

ering to chew the noodles. Lefty kept giving me meaningful glances across the table. I could see that he was as eager as I was to scare Zack.

"Where'd you get that haircut?" my mom asked Zack. She walked around the table, staring at Zack's head, frowning. I could tell she *hated* it.

"At Quick Cuts," Zack told her after swallowing a mouthful of peanut butter and jelly. "You know. At the mall."

We all studied Zack's haircut. I thought it was kind of cool. The way it was buzzed so short on the left, then hung down long on the right.

"It's different, all right," my mom said.

We all could tell she hated it. But I guess she thought she was covering up by calling it *different.* If I ever came home with a haircut like that, she'd *murder* me!

"What did your mom say about it?" she asked Zack.

Zack laughed. "Not much."

We all laughed. I kept glancing up at the clock. I was so eager to get upstairs.

"How about some chocolate cupcakes?" Mom asked when we'd finished our sandwiches.

Zack started to say yes, but I interrupted him. "Can we have dessert later? I'm kinda full."

I pushed back my chair and got up quickly, motioning for Zack to follow me. Lefty was already running to the stairs.

41

"Hey — where are you going so fast?" Mom called after us, following us into the hall.

"Uh . . . upstairs . . . to the attic," I told her.

"The attic?" She wrinkled her face, puzzled. "What's so interesting up there?"

"Uh . . . just a bunch of old magazines," I lied. "They're kind of funny. I want to show them to Zack." That was pretty fast thinking, for me. I'm usually not very quick at making up stories.

Mom stared at me. I don't think she believed me. But she turned back to the kitchen. "Have fun, guys. Don't get too dirty up there."

"We won't," I told her. I led Zack up the steep stairs. Lefty was already waiting for us in the attic.

It was about a hundred degrees hotter up there. I started to sweat the second I stepped into the room.

Zack stopped a few feet behind me and looked around. "It's just a lot of old junk. What's so interesting up here?" he asked.

"You'll see," I said mysteriously.

"This way," Lefty called eagerly, running to the little room against the far wall. He was so excited, he dropped his softball. It rolled in front of him, and he tripped over it and fell facedown on the floor with a *thud*.

"I *meant* to do that!" Lefty joked, climbing up quickly and leaping after the ball, which had rolled across the floor.

"Your brother is made of rubber or something," Zack laughed.

"Falling down is his hobby," I said. "He falls down about a hundred times a day." I wasn't exaggerating.

A few seconds later, the three of us were in the hidden room standing in front of the mirror. Even though it was a sunny afternoon, the room was as dark and shadowy as ever.

Zack turned from the mirror to me, a bewildered look on his face. "*This* is what you wanted to show me?"

"Yeah." I nodded.

"Since when are you into furniture?" he asked.

"It's an interesting mirror, don't you think?" I asked.

"No," he said. "Not too interesting."

Lefty laughed. He bounced his softball off the wall and caught it.

I was deliberately taking my time. Zack was in for the surprise of his life, but I wanted to confuse him a little bit first. He was always doing stuff like that to me. He always acted as if he knew everything there was to know, and if I were good, he'd share a little bit of his knowledge with me.

Well, now I knew something he didn't know. I wanted to stretch this moment out, make it last.

But at the same time, I couldn't wait to watch the look on Zack's face when I disappeared right in front of his eyes.

"Let's go outside," Zack said impatiently. "It's too hot up here. I brought my bike. Why don't we ride to the playground behind school, see who's there?"

"Maybe later," I replied, grinning at Lefty. I turned to my brother. "Should I show Zack our secret or not?"

Lefty grinned back at me. He shrugged.

"What secret?" Zack demanded. I knew he couldn't stand to be left out of anything. He couldn't *bear* it if anyone had a secret he didn't know about.

"What secret?" he repeated when I didn't answer.

"Show him," Lefty said, tossing up the softball.

I rubbed my chin, pretended to be thinking about it. "Well . . . okay." I motioned for Zack to stand behind me.

"You're going to make funny faces in the mirror?" Zack guessed. He shook his head. "Big deal!"

"No. That's not the secret," I told him. I stepped in front of the mirror, admiring my reflection, which stared back at me in the glass.

"Watch!" Lefty urged, stepping up beside Zack.

"I'm watching. I'm watching," Zack said impatiently.

"I'll bet you I can disappear into thin air," I told Zack.

"Yeah. Sure," he muttered.

Lefty laughed.

"How much do you want to bet?" I asked.

"Two cents," Zack said. "Is this some kind of trick mirror or something?"

"Something like that," I told him. "How about ten dollars? Bet me ten dollars?"

"Huh?"

"Forget the bet. Just show him," Lefty said, bouncing up and down impatiently.

"I have a magic kit at home," Zack said. "I can do over a thousand tricks. But it's kid stuff," he sneered.

"You don't have any tricks like this," I said confidently.

"Just get it over with so we can go outside," he grumbled.

I stepped into the center of the mirror. "Ta-daa!" I sang myself a short fanfare. Then I reached up and grabbed the light chain.

I pulled it. The lamp above the mirror flashed on, blindingly bright at first, then dimming as before.

And I was gone.

"Hey!" Zack cried. He stumbled backwards.

He actually stumbled out of shock!

Invisible, I turned away from the mirror to enjoy his stunned reaction.

"Max?" he cried out. His eyes searched the room.

Lefty was laughing his head off.

"Max?" Zack sounded really worried. "Max? How'd you do that? Where *are* you?"

"I'm right here," I said.

He jumped at the sound of my voice. Lefty laughed even harder.

I reached out and took the softball from Lefty's hand. I glanced at the reflection in the mirror. The ball seemed to float in midair.

"Here. Catch, Zack." I tossed it at him.

He was so stunned, he didn't move. The ball bounced off his chest. "Max? How do you do this trick?" he demanded.

"It isn't a trick. It's real," I said.

"Hey, wait . . ." He got a suspicious look on his face. He ran around to the back of the mirror. I guess he expected me to be hiding back there.

He looked very disappointed when he didn't see me. "Is there a trapdoor or something?" he asked. He walked back in front of the mirror, got down on his hands and knees, and started searching the floorboards for a trapdoor.

I leaned over and pulled his T-shirt up over his head.

"Hey — stop it!" he yelled, climbing angrily to his feet.

I tickled his stomach.

"Stop, Max." He squirmed away, thrashing his arms, trying to hit me. He looked really frightened now. He was breathing hard, and his face was bright red.

I pulled his T-shirt up again.

He jerked it down. "You're really invisible?" His voice rose up so high, only dogs could hear it. "Really?"

"Good trick, huh?" I said right in his ear.

He jumped and spun away. "What does it feel like? Does it feel weird?"

I didn't answer him. I crept out of the room and picked up a cardboard carton just outside the door. I carried it up to the mirror. It looked great. A carton floating all by itself.

"Put it down," Zack urged. He sounded really scared. "This is really freaking me out, Max. Stop it, okay? Come back so I can see you."

I wanted to torture him some more, but I could see he was about to lose it. Besides, I was starting to feel weird again. Sort of dizzy and lightheaded. And the bright light was hurting my eyes, starting to blind me.

"Okay, I'm coming back," I announced. "Watch."

I leaned against the mirror and reached up for the chain. I suddenly felt very tired, very weak. It took all my strength to wrap my hand around the chain.

I had the strangest sensation that the mirror was pulling me, tugging me toward it, holding me down.

With a determined burst of strength, I pulled the chain.

47

The lamp went out. The room darkened.

"Where are you? I still can't see you!" Zack cried, his voice revealing panic.

"Just chill," I told him. "It takes a few seconds. The longer I stay invisible, the longer it takes to come back." And then I added, "I think."

Staring into the blank mirror, waiting for my reflection to return, I suddenly realized that I didn't know anything at all about this mirror, about turning invisible. About coming back.

My mind suddenly whirred with all sorts of terrifying questions:

What made me think that reappearing was automatic?

What if you could only come back twice? And after the third time you went invisible, you stayed invisible?

What if the mirror was broken? What if it was locked away in this hidden room because it didn't work properly and it made people stay invisible forever?

What if I never came back?

No, that can't be, I told myself.

But the seconds were ticking by. And my body was still not visible.

I touched the mirror, rubbing my invisible hand over the smooth, cool glass.

"Max, what's taking so long?" Zack asked, his voice trembling.

"I don't know," I told him, sounding as frightened and upset as he did.

And then suddenly, I was back.

I was staring at my reflection in the mirror, watching intently, gratefully, as a wide smile crossed my face.

"Ta-*daaa!*" I sang my triumphant fanfare, turning to my still shaken friend. "Here I am!"

"Wow!" Zack exclaimed, and his mouth remained in a tight O of surprise and wonder. "Wow."

"I know," I said, grinning. "Pretty cool, huh?"

I felt very shaky, kind of trembly all over. My knees felt all weak and sweaty. You know the feeling.

But I ignored it. I wanted to enjoy my moment of glory. It wasn't often that I got to do something that Zack hadn't already done ten times.

"Amazing," Zack said, staring hard at the mirror. "I've *got* to try it!"

"Well . . ." I wasn't so sure I wanted Zack to do it. It was such a big responsibility. I mean, what if something went wrong?

"You've *got* to let me do it!" Zack insisted.

"Hey — where's Lefty?" I asked, glancing quickly around the small room.

"Huh? Lefty?" Zack's eyes searched, too.

"I was so busy being invisible, I forgot he was here," I said. And then I called, "Hey, Lefty?"

No reply.

"Lefty?"

Silence.

I walked quickly around to the back of the mirror. He wasn't there. Calling his name, I made my way to the door and peered out into the attic.

No sign of him.

"He was standing right here. In front of the mirror," Zack said, suddenly pale.

"Lefty?" I called. "Are you here? Can you hear me?"

Silence.

"Weird," Zack said.

I swallowed hard. My stomach suddenly felt as if I'd swallowed a rock.

"He was right here. Standing right here," Zack said in a shrill, frightened voice.

"Well, he's gone now," I said, staring at the dark, shadowy reflection of the mirror. "Lefty's gone."

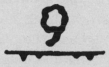

9

"Maybe Lefty went invisible, too," Zack suggested.

"Then why doesn't he answer us?" I cried. I tried calling my brother again. "Lefty — are you here? Can you hear me?"

No reply.

I walked up to the mirror and angrily slapped the frame. "Stupid mirror."

"Lefty? Lefty?" Zack had his hands cupped around his mouth like a megaphone. He stood at the door to the little room, calling out into the attic.

"I don't believe this," I said weakly. My legs were shaking so much, I dropped down onto the floor.

And then I heard giggling.

"Huh? Lefty?" I jumped to my feet.

More giggling. Coming from behind the carton I'd carried into the little room.

I lunged toward the carton just as Lefty popped

up from behind it. "Gotcha!" he cried, and collapsed over the carton, slapping the floor, laughing his head off.

"Gotcha! Gotcha both!"

"You little creep!" Zack screamed.

He and I both pounced on Lefty at the same time. I pulled his arm back until he screamed. Zack messed up his hair, then tickled him.

Lefty was screaming and laughing and squirming and crying all at the same time. I gave him a hard punch on the shoulder. "Don't ever do that again," I shouted angrily.

Lefty laughed, so I gave him a hard shove and climbed to my feet.

Zack and I, both breathing hard, both red in the face, glared angrily at Lefty. He was rolling around on the floor, covered in dust, still laughing like a lunatic.

"You scared us to death. You really did!" I exclaimed heatedly.

"I know," Lefty replied happily.

"Let's beat him up some more," Zack suggested, balling his hands into tight fists.

"Okay," I agreed.

"You'll have to catch me first!" Lefty cried. He was on his feet in a flash, and out the door.

I chased after him, tripped over a stack of old clothes, and went flying headfirst to the floor. "Ow!" I banged my leg hard. The pain shot up through my body.

Pulling myself up slowly, I started after Lefty again. But voices on the attic stairway made me stop.

Erin's head popped up first. Then April appeared.

Lefty was sitting on the windowsill at the far end of the attic, red-faced and sweaty, catching his breath.

"Hey, how's it going?" I called to the two girls, brushing dust off my jeans, then straightening my hair with one hand.

"Your mom said you were here," Erin explained, looking from Lefty to me.

"What are you guys *doing* up here?" April asked.

"Oh . . . just hanging out," I said, casting an angry glance at my brother, who stuck his tongue out in reply.

April picked up an old *Life* magazine from a stack of yellowed magazines and began flipping through it. But the pages crumbled as she looked at them. "Yuck," she said, putting it down. "This stuff is so old."

"That's what attics are for," I said, starting to feel a little more normal. "Whoever heard of keeping *new* stuff in an attic?"

"Ha-ha," Lefty laughed sarcastically.

"Where's that mirror?" Erin asked, stepping into the center of the room. "The one that made that weird optical illusion last Saturday."

"It wasn't an optical illusion," I blurted out. I didn't really feel like messing with the mirror anymore. I'd had enough scares for one afternoon. But the words just tumbled out of me.

I can never keep a secret. It's a real character flaw.

"What do you mean?" Erin asked, very interested. She walked past me, heading to the open doorway of the little room.

"You mean that wasn't an optical illusion last week?" April asked, following her.

"No, not really," I said, glancing at Lefty, who hadn't budged from the windowsill across the large room. "The mirror has strange powers or something. It really can turn you invisible."

April laughed scornfully. "Yeah. Right," she said. "And I'm going to fly to Mars in a flying saucer tonight after dinner."

"Give me a break," I muttered. I turned my eyes to Erin. "I'm serious."

Erin stared back at me, her face filled with doubt. "You're trying to tell us that you've gone in that room and become invisible?"

"I'm not *trying* to tell you," I replied heatedly. "I *am* telling you!"

April laughed.

Erin continued to stare at me, studying my face. "You *are* serious," she decided.

"It's a trick mirror," April told her. "That's all.

That light on top of it is so bright, it makes your eyes go weird."

"Show us," Erin said to me.

"Yeah. Show them!" Lefty exclaimed eagerly. He jumped up from the windowsill and started running to the little room. "I'll go this time! Let me do it!"

"No way," I said.

"Let *me* try it," Erin volunteered.

"Hey, do you know who else is here?" I asked the girls, following them to the room. "Zack is here." I called to him. "Hey, Zack. Erin wants to go invisible. Think we should let her?"

I stepped into the room. "Zack?"

"Where's he hiding?" Erin asked.

I uttered a silent gasp.

The mirror light was on. Zack was gone.

"Oh, no!" I cried. "I don't believe this!"

Lefty laughed. "Zack's invisible," he told Erin and April.

"Zack — where are you?" I demanded angrily.

Suddenly, the softball floated up from Lefty's hand. "Hey, give that back!" Lefty shouted, and grabbed for it. But invisible Zack pulled the ball out of Lefty's reach.

Erin and April were both gaping at the ball as it floated in midair, their eyes bulging, their mouths wide open.

"Hi, girls," Zack called in a booming, deep voice that floated from in front of the mirror.

April screamed and grabbed Erin's arm.

"Zack, stop kidding around. How long have you been invisible?" I asked.

"I don't know." The ball flew back to Lefty, who dropped it and had to chase it out into the attic.

"How long, Zack?" I repeated.

"About five minutes, maybe," he replied.

"When you chased after Lefty, I turned on the light and went invisible. Then I heard you talking to Erin and April."

"You've been invisible the whole time?" I asked, feeling really nervous and upset.

"Yeah. This is awesome!" he exclaimed. But then his tone grew doubtful. "I — I'm starting to feel kinda funny, though, Max."

"Funny?" Erin asked, staring at where Zack's voice seemed to be coming from. "What do you mean 'funny'?"

"Kinda dizzy," Zack replied weakly. "Everything's kind of breaking up. You know. Like a bad TV picture. I mean, you're starting to fade, to seem far away."

"I'm bringing you back," I said. And without waiting for Zack to reply, I reached up and pulled the light chain.

The light clicked off. Darkness seemed to roll into the room, filling the mirror with gray shadows.

"Where *is* he?" April cried. "It didn't work. He isn't back."

"It takes a while," I explained.

"How long?" April asked.

"I don't really know," I said.

"Why aren't I back?" Zack asked. He was standing right beside me. I could feel his breath on my neck. "I can't see myself." He sounded very frightened.

"Don't get tense," I said, forcing myself to sound calm. "You know it takes a while. Especially since you stayed invisible so long."

"But how long?" Zack wailed. "Shouldn't I be back by now? *You* were back by now. I remember."

"Just stay cool," I told him, even though my stomach was churning and my throat was dry.

"This is too scary. I *hate* this!" April moaned.

"Be patient," I repeated softly. "Everybody just be patient."

We all stared from the spot where we thought Zack was standing to the mirror, then back again.

"Zack, how do you feel?" Erin asked, her voice trembling.

"Weird," Zack replied. "Like I'm never coming back."

"Don't say that!" I snapped.

"But that's how I feel," Zack said sadly. "Like I'm never coming back."

"Just chill," I said. "Everybody. Just chill."

We stood in silence. Watching. Waiting.

Waiting.

I was never so frightened in all my life.

11

"Do something!" Zack, still invisible, pleaded. "Max — you've *got* to do something!"

"I — I'd better get Mom," Lefty stammered. He dropped the softball to the floor and started to the door.

"Mom? What could Mom do?" I cried in a panic.

"But I'd better get *somebody*!" Lefty declared.

At that moment, Zack shimmered back into view. "Wow!" He uttered a long, breathless sigh of relief and slumped to his knees on the floor.

"Yaaaay!" Erin cried happily, clapping her hands as we all gathered around Zack.

"How do you feel?" I asked, grabbing his shoulders. I think I wanted to know for sure that he was really back.

"I'm back!" Zack proclaimed, smiling. "That's all I care about."

"That was really scary," April said quietly, hands shoved into the pockets of her white tennis shorts. "I mean, really."

"I wasn't scared," Zack said, suddenly changing his tune. "I knew there was no problem."

Do you *believe* this guy?

One second, he's whining and wailing, begging me to do something.

The next second, he's pretending he had the time of his life. Mister Confident.

"What did it feel like?" Erin asked, resting one hand on the wooden mirror frame.

"Awesome," Zack replied. He climbed unsteadily to his feet. "Really. It was totally awesome! I want to get invisible again before school on Monday so I can go spy in the girls' locker room!"

"Zack, you're a pig!" Erin declared disgustedly.

"What's the point of being invisible if you can't spy on girls?" Zack asked.

"Are you sure you're okay?" I asked, genuinely concerned. "You look kind of shaky to me."

"Well, I started to feel a little strange at the end," Zack confessed, scratching the back of his head.

"How do you mean?" I asked.

"Well, like I was being pulled away. Away from the room. Away from you guys."

"Pulled where?" I demanded.

He shrugged. "I don't know. I only know one thing." A smile began to form on his face, and his blue eyes seemed to light up.

Uh-oh, I thought.

"I only know one thing," Zack repeated.

"What?" I had to ask.

"I'm the new invisible champ. I stayed invisible longer than you. At least five minutes. Longer than anybody."

"But I haven't had a turn!" Erin protested.

"I don't *want* a turn!" April declared.

"Chicken?" Zack teased her.

"I think you're stupid for messing around with this," April said heatedly. "It isn't a toy, you know. You don't know anything about it. You don't know what it really does to your body."

"I feel fine!" Zack told her, and pounded his chest with both hands like a gorilla to prove it. He glanced at the dark mirror. "I'm ready to go back — even longer."

"I want to get invisible and go outside and play tricks on people," Lefty said enthusiastically. "Can I go next, Max?"

"I — I don't think so. . . ."

I was thinking about what April had said. We really were messing around with something that could be dangerous, something we didn't know anything about.

"Max has to go again," Zack said, slapping me hard on the back, nearly sending me sprawling against the mirror. "To beat my record." He grinned at me. "Unless you're chicken, too."

"I'm *not* chicken!" I insisted. "I just think — "

"You're chicken," Zack accused, laughing scornfully. He started clucking loudly, flapping his arms like a chicken.

"*I'm* not chicken. Let *me* go," Lefty pleaded. "I can break Zack's record."

"It's my turn," Erin insisted. "You guys have all had turns. I haven't gone once yet!"

"Okay," I said with a shrug. "You go first, Erin. Then me." I was glad Erin was so eager to do it. I really didn't feel like getting invisible again just yet.

To be honest, I felt very fluttery and nervous.

"Me next!" Lefty insisted. "Me next! Me next!" He started chanting the words over and over.

I clamped my hand over his mouth. "Maybe we should all go downstairs," I suggested.

"Chicken?" Zack teased. "You're chickening out?"

"I don't know, Zack," I replied honestly. "I think — " I saw Erin staring at me. Was that disappointment on her face? Did Erin think I was a chicken, too?

"Okay," I said. "Go ahead, Erin. You go. Then I'll go. Then Lefty. We'll all beat Zack's record."

Erin and Lefty clapped. April groaned and rolled her eyes. Zack grinned.

It's no big deal, I told myself. I've done it three times already. It's perfectly painless. And if you just stay cool and wait patiently, you come right back the way you were.

"Does anyone have a watch?" Erin asked. "We need to keep time so I know what time I have to beat."

I could see that Erin was really into this competition.

Lefty seemed really excited, too. And of course Zack would compete in *anything*.

Only April was unhappy about the whole thing. She walked silently to the back of the room and sat down on the floor with her back against the wall, her arms folded over her knees.

"Hey, you're the only one with a watch," Erin called to April. "So you be the timer, okay?"

April nodded without enthusiasm. She raised her wrist and stared down at her watch. "Okay. Get ready."

Erin took a deep breath and stepped up to the mirror. She closed her eyes, reached up, and tugged the light chain.

The light came on with a bright flash. Erin disappeared.

"Oh, wow!" she cried. "This is way cool!"

"How does it feel?" April called from behind us, her eyes glancing from the mirror to her watch.

"I don't feel any different at all," Erin said. "What a great way to lose weight!"

"Fifteen seconds," April announced.

Lefty's hair suddenly stood straight up in the air. "Cut it out, Erin!" he shouted, twisting away from her invisible hands.

We heard Erin laugh from somewhere near Lefty.

Then we heard her footsteps as she walked out of the room and into the attic. We saw an old coat rise up into the air and dance around. After it dropped back into its carton, we saw an old magazine fly up and its pages appear to flip rapidly.

"This is so much fun!" Erin called to us. The magazine dropped back onto the stack. "I can't *wait* to go outside like this and really scare people!"

"One minute," April called. She hadn't moved from her sitting position against the wall.

Erin moved around the attic for a while, making things fly and float. Then she returned to the little room to admire herself in the mirror.

"I'm really invisible!" we heard her exclaim excitedly. "Just like in a movie or something!"

"Yeah. Great special effects!" I said.

"Three minutes," April announced.

Erin continued to enjoy herself until about four minutes had passed. Then her voice suddenly changed. She started to sound doubtful, frightened.

"I — I don't like this," she said. "I feel kind of strange."

April jumped to her feet and ran up to me. "Bring her back!" she demanded. "Hurry!"

I hesitated.

"Yes. Bring me back," Erin said weakly.

"But you haven't beaten my record!" Zack declared. "Are you sure — ?"

"Yes. Please. I don't feel right." Erin suddenly sounded far away.

I stepped up to the mirror and pulled the chain. The light clicked off.

We waited for Erin to return.

"How do you feel?" I asked.

"Just . . . weird," she replied. She was standing right next to me, but I still couldn't see her.

It took nearly three minutes for Erin to reappear. Three very tense minutes.

When she shimmered back into view, she shook herself like a dog shaking water off after a bath. Then she grinned at us reassuringly. "I'm okay. It was really terrific. Except for the last few seconds."

"You didn't beat my record," Zack reported happily. "You came so close. But you folded. Just like a girl."

"Hey — " Erin gave Zack a hard shove. "Stop being such a jerk."

"But you only had fifteen seconds to go, and you wimped out!" Zack told her.

"I don't care," Erin insisted, frowning angrily at him. "It was really neat. I'll beat your record next time, Zack."

"I'm going to be the winner," Lefty announced. "I'm going to stay invisible for a whole day. Maybe two!"

"Whoa!" I cried. "That might be dangerous, Lefty."

"It's Max's turn next," Zack announced. "Unless you want to forfeit."

"No way," I said, glancing at Erin. Reluctantly, I stepped up to the mirror and took a deep breath. "Okay, Zack, say good-bye to your record," I said, trying to sound calm and confident.

I didn't really want to do it, I admitted to myself. But I didn't want to look like a chicken in front of the others. For one thing, if I did wimp out, I knew that Lefty would only remind me of it twenty or thirty times a day for the rest of my life.

So I decided to go ahead and do it.

"One thing," I said to Zack. "When I call out 'ready,' that means I want to come back. So when I say 'ready,' you pull the light chain as fast as you can — okay?"

"Gotcha," Zack replied, his expression turning serious. "Don't worry. I'll bring you back instantly." He snapped his fingers. "Like that. Remember, Max, you've got to beat five minutes."

"Okay. Here goes," I said, staring at my reflection in the mirror.

I suddenly had a bad feeling about this.

A real bad feeling.

But I reached up and pulled on the light anyway.

66

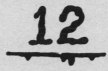

12

When the glaring light dimmed, I stared hard into the mirror.

The reflections were bright and clear. Against the back wall, I could see April, slumped on the floor, staring intently at her watch.

Lefty stood near the wall to the right, gaping at the spot where I had stood, a silly grin on his face. Zack stood next to him, his arms crossed over his chest, also staring into the mirror. Erin leaned against the wall to the left. Her eyes were on the light above the mirror frame.

And where was I?

Standing right in front of the mirror. Right in the center of it. Staring at their reflections. Staring at the spot where my reflection should be.

Only it wasn't.

I felt perfectly normal.

Experimenting, I kicked the floor. My invisible sneakers made the usual scraping sound.

I grabbed my left arm with my right hand and

squeezed it. It felt perfectly normal.

"Hi, everyone," I said. I sounded the same as ever.

Only I was invisible.

I glanced up at the light, casting a yellow rectangle down onto the mirror. What was the light's power? I wondered.

Did it do something to your molecules? Make them break apart somehow so you couldn't be seen?

No. That wasn't a good theory. If your molecules broke up, you'd *have* to feel it. And you wouldn't be able to kick the floor, or squeeze your arm, or talk.

So what did the light do? Did it cover you up somehow? Did the light form some kind of blanket? A covering that hid you from yourself and everyone else?

What a mystery!

I had the feeling I'd never be able to figure it out, never know the answer.

I turned my eyes away from the light. It was starting to hurt my eyes.

I closed my eyes, but the bright glare stayed with me. Two white circles that refused to dim.

"How do you feel, Max?" Erin's voice broke into my thoughts.

"Okay, I guess," I said. My voice sounded weird to me, kind of far away.

"Four minutes, thirty seconds," April announced.

"The time went so fast," I said.

At least, I thought I said it. I realized I couldn't tell if I was saying the words or just thinking them.

The bright yellow light glowed even brighter.

I had the sudden feeling that it was pouring over me, surrounding me.

Pulling me.

"I — I feel weird," I said.

No response.

Could they hear me?

The light folded over me. I felt myself begin to float.

It was a frightening feeling. As if I were losing control of my body.

"Ready!" I screamed. "Zack — ready! Can you hear me, Zack?"

It seemed to take Zack hours to reply. "Okay," I heard him say. His voice sounded so tiny, so far away.

Miles and miles away.

"Ready!" I cried. "Ready!"

"Okay!" Again I heard Zack's voice.

But the light was so bright, so blindingly bright. Waves of yellow light rolling over me. Ocean waves of light.

Sweeping me away with it.

"Pull the chain, Zack!" I screamed. At least, I *think* I was screaming.

The light was tugging me so hard, dragging me away, far, far away.

I knew I would float away. Float forever.

Unless Zack pulled the chain and brought me back.

"Pull it! Pull it! *Please* — pull it!"

"Okay."

I saw Zack step up to the mirror.

He was blurred in shadows. He stepped through dark shadows, on the other side of the light.

So far away.

I felt so feather light.

I could see Zack in the shadows. He jumped up. He grabbed the lamp chain.

He pulled it down hard.

The light didn't click off. It glowed even brighter.

And then I saw Zack's face fill with horror.

He held up his hand. He was trying to show me something.

He had the chain in his hand.

"Max, the chain — " he stammered. "It broke off. I can't turn off the light!"

13

Beyond the shimmering wall of yellow light, Zack's outstretched hand came clearly into my view. The dark chain dangled from his hand like a dead snake.

"It broke off!" he was crying, sounding very alarmed.

I stared through the light at the chain, feeling myself hovering beside Zack, floating, fading.

Somewhere far in the distance, April was screaming. I couldn't make out her words.

Lefty stood frozen in the center of the room. It seemed strange to see him standing so still. He was always moving, always bouncing, running, falling. But now he, too, stood staring at the chain.

The light shimmered brighter.

I saw sudden movement.

Someone was crossing the room. I struggled to focus.

It was Erin. She was dragging a large cardboard box across the floor. The scraping sound it made seemed so far away.

Feeling myself being pulled away, I struggled to watch her. She pulled the box next to the mirror. Then she climbed up onto it.

I saw her reaching up to the lamp. I saw her staring into the light.

I wanted to ask her what she was doing, but I was too far away. I was floating off. I felt so light, so feather light.

And as I floated, the yellow light spread over me. It covered me. Pulled me.

And then with startling suddenness, it was gone.

And all was darkness.

"I did it!" Erin proclaimed.

I heard her explaining to the others. "There was a little bit of chain left up there. I pulled it and turned off the light." Her eyes darted frantically around the room, searching for me. "Max — are you okay? Can you hear me?"

"Yeah. I'm okay," I replied.

I felt better. Stronger. Closer.

I stepped up to the mirror and searched for my reflection.

"That was scary," Lefty said behind me.

"I can feel myself coming back," I told them.

"What was his time?" Zack asked April.

April's features were tight with worry. Sitting

against the wall, she looked pale and uncomfortable. "Five forty-eight," she told Zack. And then quickly added, "I really think this stupid competition is a big mistake."

"You beat my record!" Zack groaned, turning to where he figured I was standing. "I don't believe it! Almost six minutes!"

"I'm going for longer than that," Lefty said, pushing past Zack and stepping up to the mirror.

"We have to fix the chain first," Erin told him. "It's too hard to keep climbing up on a box to pull that little piece of chain."

"I felt pretty strange at the end," I told them, still waiting to reappear. "The light grew brighter and brighter."

"Did you feel like you were being pulled away?" Erin asked.

"Yeah," I replied. "Like I was fading or something."

"That's how *I* started to feel," Erin cried.

"This is just so dangerous," April said, shaking her head.

I popped back.

My knees buckled and I almost fell to the floor. But I grabbed the mirror and held myself up. After a few seconds, my legs felt strong again. I took a few steps and regained my balance.

"What if we couldn't turn off the light?" April demanded, climbing to her feet, brushing the dust off the back of her jeans with both hands. "What if the chain completely broke and the light stayed on? What then?"

I shrugged. "I don't know."

"You broke my record," Zack said, making a disgusted face. "That means I have to have another turn."

"No way!" Lefty shouted. "It's my turn next!"

"None of you are listening to me!" April cried. "Answer my question. What if one of you is invisible and the light won't go out?"

"That won't happen," Zack told her. He pulled a string from his pocket. "Here. I'm going to tie this tightly to the chain." He climbed up onto the box and began to work. "Pull the string. The light goes out," he told April. "No problem."

"Which one of us is going to be first to get invisible and then go outside?" Erin asked.

"I want to go to school and terrorize Miss Hawkins," Lefty said, snickering. Miss Hawkins is his social studies teacher. "She's been terrorizing me ever since school started. Wouldn't it be cool just to sneak up behind her and say, 'Hi, Miss Hawkins'? And she'd turn around and there'd be no one there?"

"That's the best you can do?" Erin scoffed. "Lefty, where's your imagination? Don't you want to make the chalk fly out of her hand, and the chalkboard erasers fly across the room, and the wastebasket spill everything out on her desk, and her yogurt fly into her face?"

"Yeah! That's way cool!" Lefty exclaimed.

I laughed. It was a funny idea. The four of us could go around, completely invisible, doing whatever we wanted. We could wreck the whole school in ten minutes! Everyone would be screaming and running out the doors. What a goof!

"We can't do it now," Lefty said, interrupting my thoughts. "Because it's my turn to beat the record." He turned back to April, who was standing tensely by the door, pulling at a strand of her black hair, a worried frown on her face. "Ready to time me?"

"I guess," she replied, sighing.

Lefty pushed me out of the way. He stepped in front of the mirror, stared at his reflection, and reached for the string.

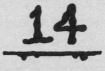

14

"Lefty!" a voice shouted from behind us. "Lefty!"

Startled by the interruption, I uttered an alarmed cry. Lefty stepped back from the mirror.

"Lefty, tell your brother his friends have to leave! It's dinnertime. Grammy and Poppy are here. They're eager to see you!"

It was Mom, calling up from downstairs.

"Okay, Mom. We'll be right down!" I shouted quickly. I didn't want her to come up.

"But that's not *fair!*" Lefty whined. "I didn't get my turn."

He stepped back up to the mirror and angrily grabbed for the string again.

"Put it down," I told him sternly. "We have to go downstairs. Quick. We don't want Mom or Dad coming up here and seeing the mirror, do we?"

"Okay, okay," Lefty grumbled. "But next time, I get to go first."

"And then me," Zack said, heading toward the stairs. "I get a chance to beat your record, Max."

"Everybody, stop talking about it," I warned as we all clomped down the stairs. "Talk about something else. We don't want them to overhear anything."

"Can we come over tomorrow?" Erin asked. "We could start up the contest again."

"I'm busy tomorrow," April said.

"We can't do it tomorrow," I replied. "We're visiting my cousins in Springfield." I was sorry they'd reminded me. My cousins have this humongous sheepdog that likes to run through the mud and then jump on me and wipe its hairy paws all over my clothes. Not my idea of a good time.

"There's no school on Wednesday," Zack said. "Teachers' meetings, I think. Maybe we could all come over on Wednesday."

"Maybe," I said.

We stepped into the hallway. Everyone stopped talking. I could see that my grandparents and parents were already sitting at the dining room table. Grammy and Poppy liked to eat promptly. If their dinner came one minute late, it made them real cranky for the rest of the day.

I ushered my friends out quickly, reminding them not to tell anyone about what we'd been doing. Zack asked again if Wednesday would be okay, and again I told him I wasn't sure.

Getting invisible was really exciting, really thrilling. But it also made me nervous. I wasn't sure I wanted to do it again so soon.

"Please!" Zack begged. He couldn't wait to get invisible again and beat my record. He couldn't stand it that he wasn't the champ.

I closed the front door behind them and hurried to the dining room to greet my grandparents. They were already slurping their soup when I came in.

"Hi, Grammy. Hi, Poppy." I walked around the table and gave them each a kiss on the cheek. Grammy smelled of oranges. Her cheek felt soft and mushy.

Grammy and Poppy are the names I gave them when I was a kid. It's really embarrassing to call them that now, but I still do. I don't have much choice. They even call *each other* Grammy and Poppy!

They look alike, almost like brother and sister. I guess that's what happens when you've been married a hundred years. They both have long, thin faces and short white hair. They both wear thick glasses with silver wire frames. They're both really skinny. And they both have sad eyes and sad expressions.

I didn't feel like sitting there at dinner and making small talk with them today. I was still really pumped about what we'd been doing all afternoon.

Being invisible was just so weird and exciting.

I wanted to be by myself and think about it. You know. Try to relive it, relive what it felt like.

A lot of times after I've done something really exciting or interesting, I like to go up to my room, lie down on my bed, and just think about it. Analyze it. Tear it apart.

Dad says I have a very scientific mind. I guess he's right.

I walked over to my place at the table.

"You're looking much shorter," Poppy said, wiping his mouth with his cloth napkin. That was one of his standard jokes. He said it every time he saw me.

I forced a laugh and sat down.

"Your soup must be ice cold by now," Grammy said, clicking her tongue. "Nothing I hate more than cold soup. I mean, what's the point of having soup if it isn't steaming hot?"

"It tastes okay," I said, taking a spoonful.

"We had some delicious cold soup last summer," Poppy said. He loved to contradict Grammy and start arguments with her. "Strawberry soup, remember? You wouldn't want *that* hot, would you?"

"It wasn't strawberry," Grammy told him, frowning. "It wasn't even soup. It was some kind of fancy yogurt."

"No, it wasn't," Poppy insisted. "It was definitely cold soup."

"You're wrong, as usual," Grammy snapped.

This could get ugly, I thought. "What kind of

soup is this?" I asked, trying to stop their arguing.

"Chicken noodle," Mom answered quickly. "Didn't you recognize it?"

"Poppy and I had soup a few weeks ago that we couldn't recognize," my grandmother said, shaking her head. "I had to ask the waiter what it was. It didn't look like what we'd ordered at all. Some kind of potato-leek soup, wasn't it, Poppy?"

Poppy took a long time swallowing some noodles. "No. Tomato," he answered.

"Where's your brother?" Dad asked, staring at the empty chair next to me.

"Huh?" I reacted with surprise. I had been so busy listening to my grandparents' silly soup arguments, I had forgotten all about Lefty.

"His soup is getting cold," Poppy said.

"You'll have to heat it up for him," Grammy said, tsk-tsking again.

"So where is he?" Dad asked.

I shrugged. "He was right behind me," I said. I turned toward the dining room doorway and shouted, "Lefty! *Lef-teeeee!*"

"Don't shout at the table," Mom scolded. "Get up and go find him."

"Is there any more soup?" Poppy asked. "I didn't really get enough."

I put my napkin down and started to get up. But before I was out of my chair, I saw Lefty's soup bowl rise up into the air.

Oh, no! I thought.

I knew instantly what was happening.

My idiot brother had made himself invisible, and now he thought he was being funny, trying to scare the daylights out of everyone at the table.

The soup bowl floated up over Lefty's place.

I stood up and lunged for it and pulled it down as fast as I could.

"Get out!" I whispered loudly to Lefty.

"What did you say?" my mom asked, gaping at me.

"I said I'm getting out and going to find Lefty," I told her, thinking quickly.

"Get out — now!" I whispered to Lefty.

"Stop talking about finding him. Just go do it," my mom said impatiently.

I stood up just as my dumb invisible brother raised his water glass. The glass floated up over the table.

I gasped and grabbed for it.

But I grabbed too hard. I jerked the glass, and water spilled all over the table.

"Hey!" Mom screamed.

I pulled the glass down to its place.

Then I looked up. Dad was glaring at me, his eyes burning angrily into mine.

He knows, I thought, a heavy feeling of dread sweeping over me.

He saw what just happened, and he knows.

Lefty has spoiled it for everyone.

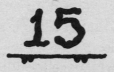

15

Dad glared angrily across the table at me.

I waited for him to say, "Max, why is your brother invisible?" But instead, he yelled, "Stop fooling around, Max. We don't appreciate your comedy act. Just get up and find your brother."

I was so relieved. Dad hadn't realized what was really happening, after all. He thought I was just goofing.

"Is there seconds on the soup?" I heard Poppy ask again as I gratefully pushed away from the table and hurried out of the dining room.

"You've had enough," Grammy scolded.

"No, I haven't!"

I made my way quickly through the living room, taking long strides, climbed to the second floor, and stopped in the hallway at the door to the attic stairs. "Lefty?" I whispered. "I hope you followed me."

"I'm here," Lefty whispered back. I couldn't see him, of course, but he was right beside me.

"What's the big idea?" I demanded angrily. I wasn't angry. I was *furious*. "Are you trying to win the *stupid* championship?"

Lefty didn't care that I was upset. He started to giggle.

"Shut up!" I whispered. "Just shut up! You really are a dork!"

I clicked on the attic light and clomped angrily up the stairs. I could hear his sneakers clomping up behind mine.

He was still giggling at the top of the stairs. "I win!" he declared. I felt a hand slap me hard on the back.

"Stop it, jerk!" I screamed, storming into the little room that housed the mirror. "Don't you realize you nearly spoiled it for everybody?"

"But I win!" he repeated gleefully.

The lamp over the mirror was shining brightly, the reflection glaring sun-yellow in the mirror.

I really couldn't believe Lefty. He was usually a pretty selfish kid. But not *this* selfish!

"Don't you realize the trouble you could have gotten us into?" I cried.

"I win! I win!" he chanted.

"Why? How long have you been invisible?" I asked. I stepped up to the mirror and pulled the string. The light went out. The glare remained in my eyes.

"Ever since you guys went downstairs," Lefty, still invisible, bragged.

"That's almost ten minutes!" I exclaimed.

"I'm the champ!" Lefty proclaimed.

I stared into the mirror, waiting for him to re-appear.

"The stupidity champ," I repeated. "This was the dumbest thing you've ever done."

He didn't say anything. Finally, he asked in a quiet voice, "Why is it taking so long for me to come back?"

Before I could answer, I heard Dad calling from downstairs: "Max? Are you two up there?"

"Yeah. We'll be right down," I shouted.

"What are you two *doing* up there?" Dad demanded. I heard him start to climb the stairs.

I ran to the top of the stairs to head him off. "Sorry, Dad," I said. "We're coming."

Dad stared up at me in the stairwell. "What on earth is so interesting up there?"

"Just a lot of old stuff," I muttered. "Nothing, really."

Lefty appeared behind me, looking like his old self. Dad disappeared back to the dining room. Lefty and I started down the stairs.

"Wow, that was *awesome*!" Lefty exclaimed.

"Didn't you start to feel weird after a while?" I asked him, whispering even though we were alone.

"No." He shook his head. "I felt fine. It was really *awesome*! You should have seen the look on your face when I made the soup bowl float up in the air!" He started giggling again, that high-pitched giggle of his that I hate.

"Listen, Lefty," I warned, stopping at the bottom of the stairs, blocking his way to the hallway. "Getting invisible is fun, but it could be dangerous. You — "

"It's awesome!" he repeated. "And I'm the new champ."

"Listen to me," I said heatedly, grabbing him by the shoulders. "Just listen. You've got to promise me that you won't go up there and get invisible by yourself again. I mean it. You've got to wait till someone else is around. Promise?" I squeezed his shoulders hard.

"Okay, okay," he said, trying to squirm away. "I promise."

I looked down. He had his fingers crossed on both hands.

Erin called me later that night. It was about eleven. I was in my pajamas, reading a book in bed, thinking about going downstairs and begging my parents to let me stay up and watch *Saturday Night Live*.

Erin sounded really excited. She didn't even say hello. Just started talking a mile a minute in that squeaky mouse voice, so fast I had trouble understanding her.

"What about the science fair?" I asked, holding the phone away from my ear, hoping that would help me understand her better.

"The winning project," Erin said breathlessly. "The prize is a silver trophy and a gift certificate at Video World. Remember?"

"Yeah. So?" I still wasn't following her. I think I was sleepier than I'd thought. It had been a nervous, tiring day, after all.

"Well, what if you brought the mirror to school?" Erin asked excitedly. "You know. I would make you go invisible. Then I'd bring you back, and I'd get invisible. That could be our project."

"But, Erin — " I started to protest.

"We'd win!" she interrupted. "We'd *have* to win! I mean, what else could beat it? We'd win first prize. And we'd be famous!"

"Whoa!" I cried. "Famous?"

"Of course. Famous!" she exclaimed. "Our picture would be in *People* magazine and everything!"

"Erin, I'm not so sure about this," I said softly, thinking hard.

"Huh? Not so sure about *what*?"

"Not so sure I want to be famous," I replied. "I mean, I really don't know if I want the whole world to know about the mirror."

"Why not?" she demanded impatiently. "*Everyone* wants to be famous. And rich."

"But they'll take away the mirror," I explained. "It's an amazing thing, Erin. I mean, is it magic? Is it electronic? Is it someone's invention? Whatever it is, it's unbelievable! And they're not going to let a kid keep it."

"But it's *yours!*" she insisted.

"They'll take it away to study it. Scientists will want it. Government guys will want it. Army guys. They'll probably want to use it to make the army invisible or something."

"Scary," Erin mumbled thoughtfully.

"Yeah. Scary," I said. "So I don't know. I've got to think about this. A lot. In the meantime, it's got to be a secret."

"Yeah, I guess," she said doubtfully. "But think about the science fair, Max. We could win the prize. We really could."

"I'll think about it," I told her.

I haven't thought about anything else! I realized.

"April wants to try it," she said.

"Huh?"

"I convinced her. I told her it didn't hurt or anything. So she wants to try it on Wednesday. We *are* going to do it on Wednesday, aren't we, Max?"

"I guess," I replied reluctantly. "Since everyone wants to."

"Great!" she exclaimed. "I think I'll beat your record."

"The new record is ten minutes," I informed her. I explained about Lefty and his dinnertime adventure.

"Your brother is really a nut," Erin remarked.

I agreed with her, then said good night.

I couldn't get to sleep that night. I tried sleeping on one side, then the other. I tried counting sheep. Everything.

I knew I was sleepy. But my heart was racing. I just couldn't get comfortable. I stared up at the ceiling, thinking about the mirror in the little room above me.

It was nearly three in the morning when I crept barefoot out of my room, wide awake, and headed up to the attic. As before, I leaned heavily on the banister as I climbed, trying to keep the wooden stairs from their usual symphony of creaks and groans.

In my hurry to get to the little room, I stubbed my toe on the corner of a wooden crate.

"Ow!" I screamed as quietly as possible. I wanted to hop up and down, but I forced myself to stand still, and waited for the pain to fade.

As soon as I could walk again, I made my way into the little room. I pulled a carton in front of the mirror and sat down on it.

My toe still throbbed, but I tried to ignore it. I stared at my dark reflection in the mirror, studying my hair first, of course. It was totally messed up, but I really didn't care.

Then I peered beyond my reflection, behind it. I guess I was trying to look deep into the glass. I don't really know what I was doing or why I was up there.

I was so tired and pumped up at the same time, so curious and confused, sleepy and nervous.

I ran a hand along the glass, surprised again at how cool it felt in the hot, nearly airless little room. I pushed my open hand against the glass, then pulled it away. It left no handprint.

I moved my hand to the wooden frame, once again rubbing the smooth wood. I stood up and slowly walked around to the back of the mirror. It was too dark back here to really examine it carefully. But there wasn't anything to examine. The back of the frame was smooth, plain, and uninteresting.

I came back around to the front and gazed up at the light. It looked like an ordinary lamp. Nothing at all special about it. The bulb was an odd shape, long and very thin. But it looked like an ordinary light bulb.

Sitting back down on the carton, I rested my head in my hands and stared drowsily into the mirror. I yawned silently.

I knew I should go back downstairs and go to sleep. Mom and Dad were going to wake us up early the next morning to drive to Springfield.

But something was holding me there.

My curiosity, I guess.

I don't know how long I sat there, still as a statue, watching my own unmoving reflection. It may have been just a minute or two. Or it might have been half an hour.

But after a while, as I stared into the mirror, the reflection seemed to lose its sharpness. Now I found myself staring at vague shapes, blurred colors, deepening shadows.

And then I heard the soft whisper.

"*Maaaaaaaax.*"

Like the wind through the trees. The hushed shaking of leaves.

Not a voice at all. Not even a whisper.

Just the hint of a whisper.

"*Maaaaaaaaax.*"

At first, I thought it was inside my own head. So faint. So soft. But so near.

I held my breath, listened hard.

Silence now.

So it *was* inside my head, I told myself. I *was* imagining it.

I took a deep breath, let it out slowly.

"*Maaaaax.*"

Again, the whisper.

Louder this time. Sad, somehow. Almost a plea. A call for help. From far, far away.

"*Maaaaaaaax.*"

I raised my hands to my ears. Was I trying to shut it out? To see if I could make it go away?

Inside the mirror, the dark reflected shapes

shifted slowly. I stared back at myself, my expression tense, frightened. I realized I was chilled from head to foot. My whole body shivered from the cold.

"Maaaaax."

The whisper, I realized, was coming from the mirror.

From my own reflection? From somewhere behind my reflection?

I leapt to my feet, turned away, and ran. My bare feet slapped against the hardwood floor. I plunged down the stairs, flew across the hall, dived into my bed.

I shut my eyes tight and prayed the frightening whisper wouldn't follow me.

16

I pulled the covers up to my chin. I felt so cold. My entire body was trembling.

I was breathing hard, gripping the top of the blanket with both hands, waiting, listening.

Would the whispers follow me into my room? Were they real, or only in my head?

Who was calling to me, whispering my name in that sad, desperate voice?

Suddenly I heard panting louder than mine. I felt hot breath on my face. Sour-smelling and moist.

It reached for me. It grabbed my face.

I opened my eyes in terror.

"Whitey!" I cried.

The dumb dog was standing on his hind paws, leaning over the blanket, furiously licking my face.

"Whitey, good dog!" I cried, laughing. His

scratchy tongue tickled. I was never so glad to see him.

I hugged him and pulled him up into the bed. He whimpered excitedly. His tail was wagging like crazy.

"Whitey, what's got you so worked up?" I asked, hugging him. "Do you hear voices, too?"

He uttered a low bark, as if answering the question. Then he hopped off the bed and shook himself. He turned three times in a tight circle, making a place for himself on the carpet, and lay down, yawning loudly.

"You're definitely weird tonight," I said. He curled himself into a tight ball and chewed softly on his tail.

Accompanied by the dog's gentle snores, I eventually drifted into a restless sleep.

When I awoke, the morning sky outside my bedroom window was still gray. The window was open just a crack, and the curtains were swaying in a strong breeze.

I sat up quickly, instantly alert. I have to stop going up to the attic, I thought.

I have to forget about the stupid mirror.

I stood up and stretched. I've got to stop. And I've got to get everyone else to stop.

I thought of the whispered cry from the night before. The dry, sad voice, whispering my name.

"Max!"

The voice from outside my room startled me out of my chilling thoughts.

"Max — time to wake up! We're going to Springfield, remember?" It was my mom out in the hallway. "Hurry. Breakfast is on the table."

"I'm already up!" I shouted. "I'll be down in a minute."

I heard her footsteps going down the stairs. Then I heard Whitey downstairs barking at the door to be let out.

I stretched again.

"Whoa!" I cried out as my closet door swung open.

A red Gap T-shirt rose up off the top shelf and began to float across the room.

I heard giggling. Familiar giggling.

The T-shirt danced in front of me.

"Lefty, you're ridiculous!" I yelled angrily. I swiped at the T-shirt, but it danced out of my reach. "You promised you wouldn't do this again!"

"I had my fingers crossed," he said, giggling.

"I don't care!" I cried. I lunged forward and grabbed the shirt. "You've got to stop. I mean it."

"I just wanted to surprise you," he said, pretending his feelings were hurt. A pair of jeans floated up from the closet shelf and began to parade back and forth in front of me.

"Lefty, I'm going to *murder* you!" I shouted. Then I lowered my voice, remembering that Mom and Dad might hear. "Put that down — now. Go upstairs and turn off the mirror light. Hurry!"

I shook my fist at where the jeans were marching. I was so angry.

Why did he have to be so dumb? Didn't he realize that this wasn't just a game?

Suddenly, the jeans collapsed in a heap on the carpet.

"Lefty, toss them to me," I instructed him. "Then get upstairs and get yourself visible again."

Silence.

The jeans didn't move.

"Lefty— don't fool around," I snapped, feeling a stab of dread in the pit of my stomach. "Toss me the jeans and get out of here."

No reply.

The jeans remained crumpled on the carpet.

"Stop this stupid game!" I screamed. "You're not funny! So just stop it. Really. You're *scaring* me!"

I knew that's what he wanted to hear. Once I admitted that he was scaring me, I was sure he'd giggle and go do as I said.

But no. The room was still silent. The curtains fluttered toward me, then pulled back with a gentle rustling sound. The jeans lay crumpled on the carpet.

"Lefty? Hey, Lefty?" I called, my voice trembling.

No reply.

"Lefty? Are you here?"

No.

Lefty was gone.

17

"Lefty?" My voice came out weak and trembling.

He wasn't there. It wasn't a game. He was gone.

Without thinking, I ran out of my room, down the hall, and up the stairs to the attic. My bare feet pounded on the steep wooden steps. My heart was pounding even louder.

As I stepped into the heat of the attic, a wave of fear swept over me.

What if Lefty had disappeared *forever*?

With a frightened cry, I lunged into the tiny room.

The bright light reflected in the mirror shone into my eyes.

Shielding my eyes with one hand, I made my way to the mirror and pulled the string. The light went out immediately.

"Lefty?" I called anxiously.

No reply.

"Lefty? Are you up here? Can you hear me?"

Fear clogged my throat. I was panting loudly, barely able to speak.

"Lefty?"

"Hi, Max. I'm here." My brother's voice came from right beside me.

I was so happy to hear it, I turned and gave him a hug, even though I couldn't see him.

"I'm okay," he said, startled by my emotion. "Really, Max. I'm okay."

It took a few minutes for him to reappear.

"What happened?" I asked, checking him out, looking him up and down as if I hadn't seen him for months. "You were clowning around in my room. Then you were gone."

"I'm fine," he insisted with a shrug.

"But where did you go?" I demanded.

"Up here," he repeated.

"But Lefty — " Something about him looked different. I couldn't quite put my finger on it. But staring at his face, I was sure that something was weird.

"Stop staring at me like that, Max." He shoved me away. "I'm fine. Really." He started dancing away from me, heading to the stairs.

"But, Lefty — " I followed him out of the room.

"No more questions. Okay? I'm all right."

"Stay away from the mirror," I said sternly. "Do you hear me?"

He started down the stairs.

"I mean it, Lefty. Don't get invisible again."

"Okay, okay," he snapped. "I won't do it anymore."

I checked to make sure his fingers weren't crossed. This time they weren't.

Mom was waiting for us in the hall. "So *there* you are," she said impatiently. "Max, you're not dressed!"

"I'll hurry," I told her, and bolted into my room.

"Lefty, what did you do to your hair?" I heard Mom ask my brother. "Did you brush it differently or something?"

"No," I heard Lefty reply. "It's the same, Mom. Really. Maybe your eyes are different."

"Stop being such a smart mouth and get downstairs," Mom told him.

Something was definitely weird about Lefty. Mom had noticed it, too. But I couldn't figure out what.

As I picked my jeans up off the floor and pulled them on, I started to feel a little better. I had been so frightened, frightened that something terrible had happened to my brother. Frightened that he'd disappeared for good, and I'd never see him again.

All because of that stupid mirror.

All because it was such a thrill to get invisible.

I suddenly thought about Erin, April, and Zack.

They were so excited about Wednesday. About the big competition. Even April was going to get invisible this time.

No, I thought.

I have to call them. I have to tell them.

I've really made up my mind.

No more mirror. No more getting invisible.

I'll call all three of them when I get back from Springfield. And I'll tell them the competition is cancelled.

I sat down on my bed to tie my sneakers.

Whew, I thought. That's a load off my mind.

And it was. Having decided not to use the mirror ever again made me feel much, much better. All of my fear seemed to float away.

Little did I know that the most frightening time was still to come.

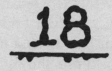

18

Imagine my surprise when Zack, Erin, and April showed up at my front door on Wednesday morning.

"I told you guys the competition is off," I sputtered, staring at them in astonishment through the screen door.

"But Lefty called us," Erin replied. "He said you changed your mind." The other two agreed.

My mouth dropped open to my knees. "Lefty?"

They nodded. "He called us yesterday," April said.

"But Lefty isn't even here this morning," I told them as they marched into the house. "He's at the playground playing softball with some of his friends."

"Who's here?" my mom called. She came walking into the hallway, drying her hands on a dish towel. She recognized my friends, then turned to me, a bewildered look on her face. "Max, I thought you were going to help me down in the basement.

101

I didn't know you'd made plans with Zack, Erin, and April."

"I didn't," I replied weakly. "Lefty — "

"We just dropped by," Zack told Mom, coming to my rescue.

"If you're busy, Max, we can go," Erin added.

"No, that's okay," Mom told them. "Max was complaining about how boring it would be to help me. It's good you three showed up."

She disappeared back into the kitchen. As soon as she was gone, my three friends practically pounced on me.

"Upstairs!" Zack cried eagerly, pointing to the stairs.

"Let's get invisible!" Erin whispered.

"I get to go first since I've never gone," April said.

I tried to argue with them, but I was outnumbered and outvoted. "Okay, okay," I reluctantly agreed. I started to follow them up the stairs when I heard scratching noises at the door.

I recognized the sound. It was Whitey, back from his morning walk. I pushed open the screen door and he trotted in, wagging his tail.

The dumb dog had some burrs stuck to his tail. I chased him into the kitchen and managed to get him to stand still long enough to pull them off. Then I hurried up to the attic to join my friends.

By the time I got up there, April was already standing in front of the mirror, and Zack was standing beside her, ready to pull the light on.

"Whoa!" I called.

They turned to look at me. I could see that April had a frightened expression on her face. "I have to do this right away. Or else I might wimp out," she explained.

"I just think we should get the rules straight first," I said sternly. "This mirror really isn't a toy, and — "

"We know, we know," Zack interrupted, grinning. "Come on, Max. No lectures today, okay? We know you're nervous because you're going to lose. But that's no reason — "

"I don't want to compete," April said nervously. "I just want to see what it's like to be invisible. For just a minute. Then I want to come back."

"Well, I'm going for the world's record," Zack boasted, leaning against the mirror frame.

"Me, too," Erin said.

"I really don't think it's a good idea," I told them, staring at my reflection in the mirror. "We should just get invisible for a short time. It's too dangerous to — "

"What a wimp!" Zack declared, shaking his head.

"We'll be careful, Max," Erin said.

"I just have a really bad feeling," I confessed. My hair was standing up in the back. I stepped closer to the mirror to see better, and smoothed it down with my hand.

"I think we should all get invisible at the same time," Zack said to me, his blue eyes lighting up with excitement. "Then we could go to the playground and scare your brother to death!"

Everyone laughed except April. "I just want to try it for a minute," she insisted. "That's all."

"First we compete," Erin told Zack. "Then we go out and scare people."

"Yeah! All *right*!" Zack exclaimed.

I decided to give up. There was no sense in trying to reason with Zack and Erin. They were too psyched for this competition. "Okay, let's get it over with," I told them.

"But first I go," April said, turning back to the mirror.

Zack reached up for the string again. "Ready? On three," he said.

I turned to the door as Whitey came sniffing his way in, his nose lowered to the floor, his tail straight out behind him.

"Whitey, what are *you* doing up here?" I asked.

He ignored me and continued sniffing furiously.

"One . . . two . . ." Zack started.

"When I say 'ready,' bring me back. Okay?" April asked, standing stiffly, staring straight ahead into the mirror. "No jokes or anything, Zack."

"No jokes," Zack replied seriously. "As soon as you want to come back, I'll turn off the light."

"Good," April replied softly.

Zack began his count again. "One . . . two . . . three!"

As he said three and pulled the string, Whitey stepped up beside April.

The light flashed on.

"Whitey!" I screamed. "Stop!"

But it was too late.

With a *yelp* of surprise, the dog vanished along with April.

19

"The dog!" Erin screamed.

"Hey — I'm gone! I'm invisible!" April exclaimed at the same time.

I could hear Whitey whimpering. He sounded really frightened.

"Pull the string!" I shouted to Zack.

"Not yet!" April protested.

"Pull it!" I insisted.

Zack pulled the string. The light went out. April reappeared first, with an angry expression on her face.

Whitey reappeared, and fell down. He jumped up quickly, but his legs were all wobbly.

He looked so funny, we all started to laugh.

"What's going on up there?" My mom's voice from the stairwell startled us into instant silence. "What are you doing?"

"Nothing, Mom," I answered quickly, signalling for my friends to remain silent. "Just hanging out."

"I don't understand what's so interesting up there in that dusty old attic," she called up.

I crossed my fingers, hoping she wouldn't come upstairs to find out.

"We just like it up here," I replied. Pretty lame, but it was the only thing I could think of to say.

Whitey, having recovered his balance, went running to the stairs. I heard the dog's toenails click on the wooden stairs as he went down to join my mom.

"That wasn't fair," April complained after Mom and Whitey were gone. "I didn't get any time."

"I think we should get out of here," I pleaded. "You see how unpredictable it is. You never know what's going to happen."

"That's sort of the fun of it," Erin insisted.

"I want another turn," April said.

We argued for about ten minutes. Once again, I lost.

It was time to start the competition. Erin was going first.

"Ten minutes is the time to beat," Zack instructed her.

"No problem," Erin said, making funny faces at herself in the mirror. "Ten minutes is too easy."

April had resumed her position, sitting on the floor with her back against the wall, studying her watch. We had agreed that she would take another turn after the competition was over.

After it was over . . .

Standing there watching Erin get ready, I wished it were over already. I felt cold all over. I had a heavy feeling of dread weighing me down.

Please, please, I thought to myself, let everything go okay.

Zack pulled the string.

Erin disappeared in the flash of light.

April studied her watch.

Zack took a step back from the mirror and crossed his arms in front of his chest. His eyes glowed with excitement.

"How do I look?" Erin teased.

"You never looked better," Zack joked.

"I like what you did with your hair," April teased, glancing up from the watch.

Even April was joking and having a good time. Why couldn't I relax, too? Why was I suddenly so frightened?

"You feel okay?" I asked Erin. The words nearly caught in my throat.

"Fine," Erin replied.

I could hear her footsteps as she walked around the room.

"If you start to feel weird, just say 'ready,' and Zack'll pull the string," I said.

"I know," she replied impatiently. "But I won't be ready to come back until I break the record."

"I'm going next," Zack told Erin, arms still crossed in front of him. "So your record won't last for long."

Suddenly Zack's arms uncrossed. His hands flew wildly up in the air, and he began slapping his face with both hands.

"Ow! Cut it out, Erin!" he yelled, trying to squirm away. "Let go!"

We heard Erin laugh as Zack slapped himself a few more times, then finally managed to wrestle out of her grip.

"One minute," April announced from behind us.

"Ow! You hurt me!" Zack said, scowling and rubbing his red cheeks.

Erin laughed again.

"You still feel okay?" I asked, glancing into the mirror.

"Fine. Stop worrying, Max," Erin scolded.

My T-shirt suddenly pulled up over my head. Erin laughed.

"Give me a break!" I cried, spinning away.

"Two minutes," April announced.

I heard the attic stairs creaking. A few seconds later, Whitey poked his head in. This time, he stopped in the doorway and peered into the room without entering.

"Go back downstairs, boy," I told him. "Go down."

He stared back at me as if considering my request. But he didn't budge from the doorway.

I didn't want to take another chance of him getting too close to the mirror. So I grabbed him by the collar and guided him to the stairs. Then it took a while for the dumb dog to get the idea that he was supposed to go *down* the stairs!

When I returned to the little room, April had just called out four minutes. Zack was pacing impatiently back and forth in front of the mirror. I guess he couldn't wait for it to be his turn.

I found myself thinking about Lefty. Lefty knew I had called everyone and canceled the competition. So why had he called Zack, Erin, and April and told them it was back on?

Just one of his practical jokes, I decided.

I'd have to find a way to pay him back for this. Something really evil . . .

"Eight minutes," April said, stretching.

"Pretty good," Zack told Erin. "Sure you don't want to quit now? There's no way you can win. Why not save everyone the time?"

"Do you still feel okay?" I asked anxiously.

No reply.

"Erin?" I called, searching around as if I had a chance of spotting her. "You feel okay?"

No reply.

"Erin — don't mess around. It's not funny!" I cried.

"Yeah. Answer us!" Zack demanded.

Still no reply.

Glancing into the mirror, I saw April's reflection, caught her horrified expression. "Erin's gone," she uttered, her voice a frightened whisper.

20

"Erin — where *are* you?" I shouted.

When she didn't reply, I ran over to the string. Just as I grabbed it, I heard footsteps outside the room. A few seconds later, a can of Coke came floating through the door.

"Miss me?" Erin asked playfully.

"You scared us to death!" I cried, my voice squeaking.

Erin laughed. "I didn't know you cared."

"That wasn't funny, Erin," Zack said sternly. For once he was agreeing with me. "You really did scare us."

"I got thirsty," Erin replied. The Coke can tilted up. We saw Coke start to pour out of it. The liquid abruptly disappeared as it flowed into Erin's mouth.

"I guess being invisible makes you really thirsty," Erin explained. "So I slipped downstairs and got a Coke."

"But you should've told us," April scolded, her

eyes turned back to her watch. "Nine minutes."

"You shouldn't go downstairs," I added heatedly. "I mean, what if my mom saw you?"

"*Saw* me?"

"Well . . . you know what I mean," I muttered.

Erin laughed. I didn't think it was funny.

Why was I the only one taking this seriously?

Erin beat Lefty's record and kept going. When April called out twelve minutes, Zack asked Erin if she wanted to come back.

No reply.

"Erin? Are you goofing on us again?" I demanded.

Still no reply.

I could feel my throat tighten once again with fear. I walked over and pulled the string. My hand was shaking as I pulled it. I prayed silently to myself that Erin would return okay.

The light went out. The three of us waited tensely for Erin to come back.

After what seemed an endless wait, she shimmered back into view. She turned quickly away from the mirror, a triumphant smile on her face. "The new champ!" she declared, raising her fists in a gesture of victory.

"You're okay?" I asked, my feeling of fear refusing to leave.

She nodded. "Just fine, worrywart." She stepped away from the mirror, walking unsteadily.

112

I stared at her. Something about her looked different.

She looked perfectly okay. Not pale or sick-looking or anything. But something was different. Her smile? Her hair? I wished I could figure out what.

"Max, pull the string." Zack's eager voice jerked me away from my thoughts. "Let's go, man. I'm going for *fifteen* minutes."

"Okay. Get ready," I said, glancing at Erin as I grabbed for the string. She flashed me a reassuring smile.

But something about her smile was different. Something.

But what?

I pulled the string. Zack vanished in the flash of bright light.

"Return of the Invisible Man!" he cried in a deep voice.

"Not so loud," I warned him. "My mom'll hear you downstairs."

Erin had lowered herself to the floor beside April. I walked over and stood over her. "You sure you're okay?" I asked. "You don't feel dizzy or weird or anything?"

She shook her head. "No. Really. Why don't you believe me, Max?"

As I stared down at her, I tried to figure out what was different about her appearance. What a mystery! I just couldn't put my finger on it.

"Well, how come you didn't answer when I called you?" I demanded.

"Huh?" Her face filled with surprise. "When?"

"At about twelve minutes," I told her. "I called you and Zack called you. But you didn't answer us."

Erin's expression turned thoughtful. "I guess I didn't hear you," she replied finally. "But I'm fine, Max. Really. I feel great. It was really awesome."

I joined them on the floor and leaned back against the wall to wait for Zack's turn to be over. "I really mean it. Don't turn off the light till fifteen minutes," he reminded me.

Then he messed up my hair, making it stand straight up in the air.

Both girls laughed.

I had to get up, walk over to the mirror, and comb it back down. I don't know why people think messed-up hair is such a riot. I really don't get it.

"Hey, follow me. I've got an idea," Zack said. His voice was coming from the doorway.

"Whoa — hold on!" I called. But I could hear his sneakers clomping across the attic.

"Follow me outside," he called to us. We heard his footsteps on the attic stairs.

"Zack — don't do it," I pleaded. "Whatever it is, don't do it!"

But there was no way he was going to listen to me.

A few seconds later, we were out the back door, following our invisible friend toward our neighbor Mr. Evander's back yard.

This is going to be trouble, I thought unhappily. Big trouble.

Erin, April, and I hid behind the hedge that separated our two yards. As usual, Mr. Evander was out in his tomato garden, stooped over, pulling up weeds, his big belly hanging out under his T-shirt, his red bald head shiny under the sun.

What is Zack going to do? I wondered, holding my breath, my whole body heavy with dread.

And then I saw three tomatoes float up from the ground. They hovered in the air, then floated closer to Mr. Evander.

Oh, no, I thought, groaning silently to myself. Please, Zack. Please don't do it.

Erin, April, and I were huddled together behind the hedge, staring in disbelief as the three tomatoes began to circle each other rapidly in the air.

Invisible Zack was juggling them. Showing off, as usual. He was always bragging about how he could juggle, and we couldn't.

It took a while for Mr. Evander to notice.

But when he finally saw the three tomatoes spinning around in midair a few feet in front of him, his eyes bugged out and his face turned as red as the tomatoes!

"Oh!" he cried. He let the weeds fall from his

hands. And then he just stared at the spinning tomatoes, like he was frozen.

Zack tossed the tomatoes higher as he juggled.

April and Erin held hands over their mouths to stifle their laughter. They thought Zack's stunt was a real hoot. But I just wanted to get Zack back up to the attic.

"Hey, Mary! Mary!" Mr. Evander started calling to his wife. "Mary — come out here! You've *got* to see this! Mary!"

A few seconds later, his wife came running across the yard, a frightened expression on her face. "Mike, what's wrong? What's *wrong?*"

"Look — these tomatoes are twirling in the air!" Mr. Evander cried, motioning wildly for her to hurry.

Zack let the tomatoes fall to the ground.

"Where?" Mrs. Evander asked breathlessly, running as fast as she could.

"There. Look!" Mr. Evander pointed.

"I don't see any tomatoes," Mrs. Evander said, stopping in front of her husband, panting loudly.

"Yes! They're spinning. They're — "

"Those tomatoes?" Mrs. Evander asked, pointing to the three tomatoes on the ground.

"Well . . . yes. They were twirling around, and — " Looking terribly confused, Mr. Evander scratched the back of his neck.

"Mike, how long have you been out in the sun?" his wife scolded. "Didn't I tell you to wear a cap?"

"Uh . . . I'll be in in a few minutes," Mr. Evander said softly, staring down at the tomatoes.

As soon as Mrs. Evander turned and headed back to the house, the three tomatoes floated up from the ground and began twirling in the air again.

"Mary, look!" Mr. Evander shouted excitedly. "Look — quick! They're doing it again!"

Zack let the tomatoes drop to the ground.

Mrs. Evander spun around and stared into empty space. "Mike, you'd better come with me — *right now*," she insisted. She hurried back, grabbed Mr. Evander by the arm, and pulled him away. The poor man looked totally bewildered, staring at the tomatoes on the ground, still scratching the back of his neck as his wife pulled him to the house.

"Hey, this is awesome!" Zack cried, right in front of me.

Erin and April collapsed in wild giggles. I had to admit it was pretty funny. We laughed about it for a while. Then we sneaked back into the house and up to the attic.

In the safety of the little room, we laughed some more about Zack's juggling stunt. Zack bragged that he was the world's first invisible juggler.

Then, at twelve minutes, Zack suddenly stopped answering us.

Just as Erin had.

The three of us called his name over and over.

Silence.

Zack didn't reply.

"I'm going to bring him back," I said, instantly gripped with fear once again. I ran to the string.

"Wait," Erin said, holding me back.

"Huh? What for?" I pulled away from her.

"He said to wait till fifteen minutes, remember?" she argued.

"Erin, he's completely disappeared!" I cried.

"But he'll be really mad," Erin pleaded.

"I say bring him back," April said anxiously.

"Give him until fifteen minutes," Erin insisted.

"No," I said. I pulled the string.

The light clicked off.

A few minutes later, Zack flickered back. He smiled at us. "How long?" he asked, turning to April.

"Thirteen minutes, twenty seconds," she told him.

His grin widened. "The new champ!"

"You're okay? You didn't answer us," I said, studying his face.

"I'm fine. I didn't hear you calling me. But I'm fine."

Zack looked different to me, too. Something was very different about him. But what?

"What's your problem, Max?" he demanded. "Why are you staring at me like I'm some kind of alien life-form or something?"

"Your hair," I said, studying him. "Was it like that before?"

"Huh? What are you talking about? Are you freaking out or something?" Zack asked, rolling his eyes.

"Was your hair like that before?" I repeated. "Buzzed real short on the right and then combed long to the left? Wasn't it the other way around?"

"You're messed up, Max," he said, grinning at Erin and April. "My hair is the same it's always been. You've been staring in that mirror too long or something."

I could've sworn his hair had been short on the left, long on the right. But I guess Zack would know his own hair.

"Are you going to go?" Erin asked, jumping up behind me.

"Yeah, are you going to beat fifteen minutes?" Zack asked.

I shook my head. "No, I really don't feel like it," I told them truthfully. "Let's declare Zack the winner and get out of here."

"No way!" Zack and Erin declared in unison.

"You've got to try," Zack insisted.

"Don't wimp out, Max. You can beat Zack. I know you can," Erin declared.

She and Zack both pushed me up to the mirror.

I tried to pull back. But they practically held me in place.

"No. Really," I said. "Zack can be the winner. I — "

"Go for it, Max!" Erin urged. "I'm betting on you!"

"Yeah. Go for it," Zack repeated, his hand firmly on my shoulder.

"No. Please — " I said.

But Zack reached up with his free hand and pulled the string.

21

I stared into the mirror for a moment, waiting for the glare to fade from my eyes. It was always such a shock. That first moment, when your reflection disappeared. When you stared at the spot where you knew you were standing — and realized you were looking right through yourself!

"How do you feel, Max? How do you feel?" Erin asked, imitating me.

"Erin, what's your problem?" I snapped. It wasn't like her to be so sarcastic.

"Just giving you a taste of your own medicine," she replied, grinning.

Something about her smile was lopsided, not normal.

"Think you can beat my record?" Zack demanded.

"I don't know. Maybe," I replied uncertainly.

Zack stepped up to the mirror and studied his reflection. I had the strangest feeling as I watched him. I can't really explain it. I'd never seen Zack stand in just that position and admire himself in just that way.

Something was different. I knew it. But I couldn't figure out what.

Maybe it's just my nervousness, I told myself. I'm just so stressed out. Maybe it's affecting the way I look at my friends. Maybe I'm making all this up.

"Two minutes," April announced.

"Are you just going to stand there?" Erin asked, staring into the mirror. "Aren't you going to move around or anything, Max?"

"No. I don't think so," I said. "I mean, I can't think of anything I want to do. I'm just going to wait till the time is up."

"You want to quit now?" Zack asked, grinning at the spot where he thought I was standing.

I shook my head. Then I remembered that no one could see it. "No. I might as well go the distance," I told him. "Since I'm here, I might as well make you look bad, Zack."

He laughed scornfully. "You won't beat thirteen-twenty," he said confidently. "No way."

"Well, you know what?" I said, angered by his smug tone of voice. "I'm just going to stand here until I do."

And that's what I did. I stood in place, leaning against the mirror frame, while April counted off the minutes.

I did okay until a short while after she had called

out eleven minutes. Then, suddenly, the glare of the light began to hurt my eyes.

I closed my eyes, but it didn't help. The light grew brighter, harsher. It seemed to sweep around me, surround me, fold over me.

And then I began to feel dizzy and light. As if I were about to float away, even though I knew I was standing in place.

"Hey, guys?" I called out. "I think I've had enough."

My voice sounded tiny and far away, even to me.

The light swirled around me. I felt myself grow lighter, lighter, until I had to struggle to keep my feet on the floor to keep from floating away.

I uttered a high-pitched cry. I was suddenly gripped by panic.

Cold panic.

"Zack — bring me back!" I shouted.

"Okay, Max. No problem," I heard Zack reply.

He seemed miles and miles away.

I struggled to see him through the blinding yellow light. He was a dark figure behind the wall of light, a dark figure moving quickly to the mirror.

"I'm bringing you back now, Max. Hold on," I heard Zack say.

The bright light glowed even brighter. It hurt so much. Even with my eyes closed, it hurt.

"Zack, pull the string!" I shouted.

I opened my eyes to see his dim shadow reaching up to the string.

Pull it, pull it, *pull it*! I urged silently.

I knew that in a second, the light would go off. And I'd be safe.

A second.

One tug of the string.

Pull it, pull it, *pull it, Zack!*

Zack reached for the string. I saw him grab it.

And then I heard another voice in the room. A new voice. A surprised voice.

"Hi. What's going on up here? What are you kids doing?"

I saw the shadowy figure of Zack drop the string and step away without pulling it.

My mom had burst into the room.

22

"Please — pull the string!" I called.

No one seemed to hear me.

"We're just hanging out," I heard Zack tell my mom.

"But where's Max?" I heard her ask. "How did you find this little room? What are you all *doing* in here?" Her voice sounded as if it were coming from underwater, far, far away.

The entire room began to shimmer in the light, flickering on and off. I held on tightly to the frame of the mirror, struggling not to float away.

"Can you hear me?" I called. "Please, some-body — pull the string! Bring me back!"

They were just gray shadows in the wavering, rolling light. They didn't seem to hear me.

Gripping the frame tightly, I saw a shadow approach the mirror. My mom. She walked around it, admiring it.

"I can't *believe* we never knew about this room.

Where did this old mirror come from?" I heard her ask.

She was standing so close to me. They all were.

They were so close and so far away at the same time.

"Please bring me back!" I shouted.

I listened for an answer. But the voices faded away.

The shadows moved in a flickering blur. I tried to reach out to them, but they were too far away.

I let go of the mirror frame and began to float.

"Mom, I'm right here. Can't you hear me? Can't you *do* anything?"

So light, so completely weightless, I floated in front of the mirror.

My feet were off the floor. I couldn't see them in the blinding glare.

I floated to the mirror glass, under the light.

I could feel the light pull me closer. Closer.

Until it pulled me right into the mirror.

I knew I was inside the mirror. Inside a glistening blur of colors. The shapes shimmered and rolled together as if underwater.

And I floated through the glimmering shards of light and color, floated silently away from my friends, away from my mom, floated away from the tiny attic room.

Into the center of the mirror.

Into the center of an undulating, rolling world of twisting lights and colors.

"Help me!" I cried.

But my voice was muffled by the blurred, shifting colors.

"Bring me back! Get me back!"

Floating deeper into this glimmering world, I could barely hear myself.

Deeper into the mirror. And still deeper.

The colors gave way to shapes of gray and black. It was cold here. Cold as glass.

And as I floated deeper, deeper, the grays and blacks faded, too. The world was white now. Pure white all around. Shadowless white as far as I could see.

I stared straight ahead, no longer calling out, too frightened to call out, too mystified by the cold, ivory world I had entered.

"Hello, Max," a familiar voice said.

"Ohh!" I cried out, realizing I was not alone.

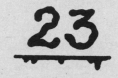

23

A scream of terror escaped my lips. I tried to form words, but my brain seemed to be paralyzed.

The figure approached quickly, silently, through the cold, white world of the mirror. He smiled at me, an eerie, familiar smile.

"You!" I managed to scream.

He stopped inches away from me.

I stared at him in disbelief.

I was staring at myself. Me. Smiling back at me. The smile as cold as the glass that surrounded us.

"Don't be afraid," he said. "I'm your reflection."

"No!"

His eyes — *my* eyes — studied me hungrily, like a dog staring at a meaty bone. His smile grew wider as I cried out my fear.

"I've been waiting here for you," my reflection said, his eyes locked on mine.

"No!" I repeated.

I turned away.

I knew I had to get away.

I started to run.

But I stopped short when I saw the faces in front of me. Distorted, unhappy faces, dozens of them, fun house mirror faces, with enormous, drooping eyes, and tiny mouths tight with sadness.

The faces seemed to hover just ahead of me. The gaping eyes staring at me, the tiny mouths moving rapidly as if calling to me, warning me, telling me to get away.

Who were these people, these faces?

Why were they inside the mirror with me?

Why did their distorted, twisted images reveal so much sadness, so much pain?

"No!"

I gasped as I thought I recognized two of the floating faces, their mouths working furiously, their eyebrows rising wildly up and down.

Erin and Zack?

No.

That was impossible, wasn't it?

I stared hard at them. Why were they talking so frantically? What were they trying to tell me?

"Help me!" I called. But they didn't seem to hear me.

The faces, dozens of them, bobbed and floated.

"Help me — please!"

And then I felt myself being spun around. I stared into the eyes of my reflection as he gripped my shoulders and held me in place.

"You're not leaving," he told me. His quiet voice echoed through the clear stillness, icicles scratching against glass.

I struggled to free myself, but his grip was strong.

"I'm the one to leave," he told me. "I've been waiting so long. Ever since you turned on the light. And now I'm going to step out from here and join the others."

"Others?" I cried.

"Your friends gave in easily," he said. "They did not resist. The switch was made. And now you and I will also make a switch."

"No!" I screamed, and my cry seemed to echo through the icy cold for miles.

"Why are you so afraid?" he asked, turning me around, still gripping my shoulders, bringing his face close to mine. "Are you so afraid of your other side, Max?"

He stared at me intently. "That's what I am, you know," he said. "I am your reflection. Your other side. Your cold side. Don't be afraid of me. Your friends were not afraid. They made the switch without much of a struggle. Now they are inside the mirror. And their reflections . . ."

His voice trailed off. He didn't have to finish his sentence. I knew what he was saying.

Now I understood about Erin and Zack. Now I understood why they looked different to me.

They were reversed. They were their own reflections.

And now I understood why they pushed me into the mirror, why they forced me to disappear, too.

If I didn't do something, I realized, my reflection would switch places with me. My reflection would step into the attic. And I'd be trapped inside the mirror forever, trapped forever with the sad, bobbing faces.

But what could I do?

Staring at myself, I decided to stall, to ask questions, to give myself a little time to think.

"Whose mirror is it? Who built it?" I demanded.

He shrugged. "How should I know? I'm only your reflection, remember?"

"But how — "

"It's time," he said eagerly. "Don't try to stall with foolish questions. Time to make the switch. Time for *you* to become *my* reflection!"

24

I pulled away.

I started to run.

The sad, distorted faces hovered in front of me.

I shut my eyes and dodged away from them.

I couldn't think. Couldn't breathe.

My legs pumped. My arms flew out at my sides. It was so clear and bright, I couldn't tell if I was moving or not. My feet couldn't feel a floor. There were no walls, no ceiling. There was no *air* brushing my face as I ran.

But my fear kept me moving. Through the clear, cold, shimmering light.

He was behind me.

I couldn't hear him.

He had no shadow.

But I knew he was right behind me.

And I knew that if he caught me, I'd be lost. Lost inside this blank world, unable to see, to hear, to smell, to touch anything, lost in the cold glass forever.

Another silent, bobbing face.

And so I kept running.

Until the colors returned.

Until light bent to form shapes.

And I saw shadows moving and shifting in front of me.

"Stop, Max!" I heard my reflection's voice right behind me. "Stop right there!"

But now *he* sounded worried.

And so I kept running, running into the colors and moving shapes.

Suddenly, Zack turned off the light.

I came bursting out of the mirror, into the tiny attic room, into an explosion of sound, of color, of hard surfaces, of real things. The real world.

I stood up, panting, gasping for breath. I tested my legs. I stomped on the floor. The solid floor.

I turned my eyes to my friends, who were standing in front of me, startled expressions on their faces. My mom, I realized, must have retreated back downstairs.

"Did you make the switch?" Zack asked eagerly, his eyes glowing with excitement.

"Are you one of us?" Erin asked at the same time.

"No," said a voice — my voice — coming from just behind me.

We all stared into the mirror.

Inside it, my reflection, red-faced and angry, glared out at us, his hands pressed against the glass. "He got away," my reflection told my friends. "The switch wasn't made."

"I don't understand!" I heard April cry. "What's going on, guys?"

Zack and Erin ignored her. They stepped up quickly and grabbed me by the arms. They spun me around roughly.

"The switch wasn't made," my reflection repeated from inside the glass.

"No problem," Erin told it.

She and Zack forced me up to the mirror.

"You're going back in, Max," Zack said heatedly.

He reached up and pulled the light cord.

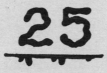

25

The light flashed on.

I went invisible.

My reflection remained in the mirror, open palms pressed against the inside of the glass, staring out.

"I'm waiting for you, Max," he said. "In a few minutes, you'll join me in here."

"No!" I shouted. "I'm leaving. I'm going downstairs."

"No, you're not," my reflection said, shaking his head. "Erin and Zack won't let you escape. But don't be so frightened, Max. It's all quite painless. Really." He smiled. It was my smile. But it was cold. Cruel.

"I don't get this," April was protesting back by the door. "Will someone tell me what's going on?"

"You'll see, April," Erin told her soothingly.

What am I going to do? I wondered, frozen in panic.

What *can* I do?

"Just a few more minutes," my reflection said calmly, already celebrating his victory. His freedom.

"April, get help!" I cried.

She spun around at the sound of my voice. "Huh?"

"Get help! Go downstairs. Get help! Hurry!" I screamed.

"But — I don't understand —" April hesitated.

Erin and Zack moved to block her path.

But the door suddenly swung open.

I saw Lefty stop at the doorway. He peered in. Saw my reflection.

He must have thought the reflection was me.

"Think fast!" he shouted, and he tossed a softball.

The ball smashed into the mirror.

I saw the startled look on Lefty's face. And then I heard the crash and saw the mirror crack and shatter.

My reflection didn't have time to react. He broke into shards of glass and fell to the floor.

"Nooooo!" Erin and Zack shrieked.

I popped back into view just as Erin's and Zack's reflections floated up off the floor. They were sucked into the broken mirror — screaming all the way — sucked into it as if a powerful vacuum cleaner were pulling them in.

The two reflections flew screaming into the mirror and appeared to crack into hundreds of pieces.

"Whoa!" Lefty cried, gripping the door with all his strength, pressing his body against the doorframe, struggling to keep himself from being sucked into the room.

And then Erin and Zack dropped onto the floor on their knees, looking dazed and confused, staring at the pieces of shattered mirror that littered the floor around them.

"You're back!" I cried happily. "It's really you!"

"Yeah. It's me," Zack said, climbing unsteadily to his feet, then turning to help Erin up.

The mirror was shattered. The reflections were gone.

Erin and Zack gazed around the room, still shaken and dazed.

April stared at me in total confusion.

Lefty remained outside the doorway, shaking his head. "Max," he said, "you should've caught the ball. That was an easy catch."

Erin and Zack were back. And they were okay.

It didn't take long to get everything back to normal.

We explained everything to April and Lefty as best we could.

April went home. She had to baby-sit her little sister.

Erin and Zack — the *real* Erin and Zack — helped me sweep up the broken glass. Then we closed the door to the little room. I latched it tightly, and we all carried cartons over and stacked them up to block off the door.

We knew we'd never go in there again.

We vowed never to tell anyone about getting invisible or the mirror or what happened in that little room. Then Erin and Zack headed home.

Later, Lefty and I were hanging around out in the back yard. "That was so scary," I told Lefty with a shudder. "You just can't imagine what it was like."

"Sounds pretty scary," Lefty replied absently. He tossed his softball from hand to hand. "But at least everything is okay now. Want to play a little catch?"

"No," I shook my head. I wasn't in the mood. But then I changed my mind. "Maybe it'll take my mind off what happened this morning," I said.

Lefty tossed me the ball. We trotted behind the garage, our usual place for tossing the ball around.

I lobbed it back to him.

We were having a pretty good game of catch.

Until about five minutes had gone by.

Until . . .

Until I stopped and froze in place.

Were my eyes playing tricks on me?

"Here comes my fastball," he said. He heaved it at me.

No. No. No.

I gaped open-mouthed as the ball shot past me.
I didn't even try to catch it. I couldn't move.
I could only stare in horror.

My brother was throwing right-handed.

Add *more*

Goosebumps

to your collection . . .
A chilling preview of
what's next from
R.L. STINE

NIGHT OF THE LIVING DUMMY

2

A child?

Kris uttered a silent gasp, staring in horror as Lindy lifted it out of the trash Dumpster.

She could see his face, frozen in a wide-eyed stare. His brown hair stood stiffly on top of his head. He seemed to be wearing some sort of gray suit.

His arms and legs dangled lifelessly.

"Lindy!" Kris called, her throat tight with fear. "Is it — is he . . . *alive?*"

Her heart pounding, Kris started to run to her sister. Lindy was cradling the poor thing in her arms.

"Is he alive?" Kris repeated breathlessly.

She stopped short when her sister started to laugh.

"No. Not alive!" Lindy called gleefully.

And then Kris realized that it wasn't a child after all. "A dummy!" she shrieked.

Lindy held it up. "A ventriloquist's dummy,"

she said. "Someone threw it out. Do you believe it? It's in perfect shape."

It took Lindy a while to notice that Kris was breathing hard, her face bright red. "Kris, what's your problem? Oh, wow. Did you think it was a real kid?" Lindy laughed scornfully.

"No. Of course not," Kris insisted.

Lindy held the dummy up and examined its back, looking for the string to pull to make its mouth move. "I *am* a real kid!" Lindy made it say. She was speaking in a high-pitched voice through gritted teeth, trying not to move her lips.

"Dumb," Kris said, rolling her eyes.

"I am *not* dumb. You're dumb!" Lindy made the dummy say in a high, squeaky voice. When she pulled the string in its back, the wooden lips moved up and down, clicking as they moved. She moved her hand up its back and found the control to make its painted eyes shift from side to side.

"It's probably filled with bugs," Kris said, making a disgusted face. "Throw it back, Lindy."

"No way," Lindy insisted, rubbing her hand tenderly over the dummy's wooden hair. "I'm keeping him."

"She's keeping me," she made the dummy say.

Kris stared suspiciously at the dummy. Its brown hair was painted on its head. Its blue eyes moved only from side to side and couldn't blink. It had bright red painted lips, curved up into an eerie smile. The lower lip had a chip on one side so that it didn't quite match the upper lip.

The dummy wore a gray, double-breasted suit over a white shirt collar. The collar wasn't attached to a shirt. Instead, the dummy's wooden chest was painted white. Big brown leather shoes were attached to the ends of its thin, dangling legs.

"My name is Slappy," Lindy made the dummy say, moving its grinning mouth up and down.

"Dumb," Kris repeated, shaking her head. "Why Slappy?"

"Come over here and I'll slap you!" Lindy made it say, trying not to move her lips.

Kris groaned. "Are we going to ride our bikes to the playground or not, Lindy?"

"Afraid poor Robby misses you?" Lindy made Slappy ask.

"Put that ugly thing down," Kris replied impatiently.

"I'm not ugly," Slappy said in Lindy's squeaky voice, sliding his eyes from side to side. "You're ugly!"

"Your lips are moving," Kris told Lindy. "You're a lousy ventriloquist."

"I'll get better," Lindy insisted.

"You mean you're really keeping it?" Kris cried.

"I like Slappy. He's cute," Lindy said, cuddling the dummy against the front of her T-shirt.

"I'm cute," she made him say. "And you're ugly."

"Shut up," Kris snapped to the dummy.

"You shut up!" Slappy replied in Lindy's tight, high-pitched voice.

"What do you want to keep it for?" Kris asked, following her sister toward the street.

"I always liked puppets," Lindy recalled. "Remember those marionettes I used to have? I played with them for hours at a time. I made up long plays with them."

"I always played with the marionettes, too," Kris remembered.

"You got the strings all tangled up," Lindy said, frowning. "You weren't any good at it."

"But what are you going to *do* with this dummy?" Kris demanded.

"I don't know. Maybe I'll work up an act," Lindy said thoughtfully, shifting Slappy to her other arm. "I'll bet I could earn some money with him. You know. Appear at kids' birthday parties. Put on shows."

"Happy birthday!" she made Slappy declare. "Hand over some money!"

Kris didn't laugh.

The two girls walked along the street in front of their house. Lindy cradled Slappy in her arms, one hand up his back.

"I think he's creepy," Kris said, kicking a large pebble across the street. "You should put him back in the Dumpster."

"No way," Lindy insisted.

"No way," she made Slappy say, shaking his head, his glassy blue eyes moving from side to side. "I'll put *you* in the Dumpster!"

"Slappy sure is mean," Kris remarked, frowning at Lindy.

Lindy laughed. "Don't look at me," she teased. "Complain to Slappy."

Kris scowled.

"You're jealous," Lindy said. "Because I found him and you didn't."

Kris started to protest, but they both heard voices. Kris looked up to see the two Marshall kids from down the block running toward them. They were cute, red-headed kids that Lindy and Kris sometimes baby-sat.

"What's that?" Amy Marshall asked, pointing at Slappy.

"Does he talk?" her younger brother, Ben, asked, staying several feet away, an uncertain expression on his freckled face.

"Hi, I'm Slappy!" Lindy made the dummy call out. She cradled Slappy in one arm, making him sit up straight, his arms dangling at his sides.

"Where'd you get him?" Amy asked.

"Do his eyes move?" Ben asked, still hanging back.

"Do *your* eyes move?" Slappy asked Ben.

Both Marshall kids laughed. Ben forgot his reluctance. He stepped up and grabbed Slappy's hand.

"Ouch! Not so hard!" Slappy cried.

Ben dropped the hand with a gasp. Then he and Amy collapsed in gleeful laughter.

"Ha-ha-ha-ha!" Lindy made Slappy laugh, tilting his head back and opening his mouth wide.

The two kids thought that was a riot. They laughed even harder.

Pleased by the response she was getting, Lindy glanced at her sister. Kris was sitting on the curb, cradling her head in her hands, a dejected look on her face.

She's jealous, Lindy realized. Kris sees that the kids really like Slappy and that I'm getting all the attention. And she's totally jealous.

I'm *definitely* keeping Slappy! Lindy told herself, secretly pleased at her little triumph.

She stared into the dummy's bright blue painted eyes. To her surprise, the dummy seemed to be staring back at her, a twinkle of sunlight in its eyes, its grin wide and knowing.

4

"Ow!"

Kris screamed and raised her hand to her cheek, which was bright pink. She stepped back. "Stop it, Lindy! That *hurt!*"

"Me?" Lindy cried. "I didn't do it! Slappy did!"

"Don't be dumb," Kris protested, rubbing her cheek. "You really hurt me."

"But I didn't do it!" Lindy cried. She turned Slappy's face toward her. "Why were you so rude to Kris?"

Mr. Powell jumped up from the couch. "Stop acting dumb and apologize to your sister," he ordered.

Lindy bowed Slappy's head. "I'm sorry," she made the dummy say.

"No. In your own voice," Mr. Powell insisted, crossing his arms in front of his chest. "Slappy didn't hurt Kris. You did."

"Okay, okay," Lindy muttered, blushing. She

avoided Kris's angry stare. "I'm sorry. Here." She dumped Slappy into Kris's arms.

Kris was so surprised, she nearly dropped the dummy. Slappy was heavier than she'd imagined.

"Now what am I supposed to do with him?" Kris asked Lindy.

Lindy shrugged and crossed the room to the couch, where she dropped down beside her mother.

"Why'd you make such a fuss?" Mrs. Powell whispered, leaning close to Lindy. "That was so babyish."

Lindy blushed. "Slappy is *mine*! Why can't something be mine for once?"

"Sometimes you girls are so nice to each other, and sometimes . . ." Mrs. Powell's voice trailed off.

Mr. Powell took a seat on the padded arm of the chair across the room.

"How do I make his mouth work?" Kris asked, tilting the dummy upside down to examine its back.

"There's a string in his back, inside the slit in his jacket," Lindy told her grudgingly. "You just pull it."

I don't want Kris to work Slappy, Lindy thought unhappily.

I don't want to share Slappy.

Why can't I have something that just belongs

to me? Why do I have to share everything with her?

Why does Kris always want to copy me?

She gritted her teeth and waited for her anger to fade.

Later that night, Kris sat straight up in bed. She'd had a bad dream.

I was being chased, she remembered, her heart still pounding. Chased by what? By whom?

She couldn't remember.

She glanced around the shadowy room, waiting for her heartbeat to return to normal. The room felt hot and stuffy, even though the window was open and the curtains were fluttering.

Lindy lay sound asleep on her side in the twin bed next to Kris's. She was snoring softly, her lips slightly parted, her long hair falling loose about her face.

Kris glanced at the clock radio on the bedtable between the two twin beds. It was nearly three in the morning.

Even though she was now wide awake, the nightmare wouldn't completely fade away. She still felt uncomfortable, a little frightened, as if she were still being chased by someone or something. The back of her neck felt hot and prickly.

She turned and fluffed up her pillow, propping it higher on the headboard. As she lay back on it, something caught her eye.

Someone sitting in the chair in front of the bedroom window. Someone staring at her.

After a sharp intake of breath, she realized it was Slappy.

Yellow moonlight poured over him, making his staring eyes glow. He was sitting up in the chair, tilted to the right at a slight angle, one arm resting on the slender arm of the chair.

His mouth locked in a wide, mocking grin, his eyes seemed to be staring right at Kris.

Kris stared back, studying the dummy's expression in the eerie yellow moonlight. Then, without thinking, without even realizing what she was doing, she climbed silently out of bed.

Her foot got tangled in the bedsheet and she nearly tripped. Kicking the sheet away, she made her way quickly across the room to the window.

Slappy stared up at her as her shadow fell over him. His grin seemed to grow wider as Kris leaned closer.

A gust of wind made the soft curtains flutter against her face. Kris pushed them away and peered down at the dummy's painted head.

She reached a hand out and rubbed his wooden hair, shining in the moonlight. His head felt warm, warmer than she'd imagined.

Kris quickly jerked her hand away.

What was that sound?

Had Slappy snickered? Had he laughed at her? No. Of course not.

Kris realized she was breathing hard.

Why am I so freaked out by this stupid dummy? she thought.

In the bed behind her, Lindy made a gurgling sound and rolled onto her back.

Kris stared hard into Slappy's big eyes, gleaming in the light from the window. She waited for him to blink or to roll his eyes from side to side.

She suddenly felt foolish.

It's just a stupid wooden dummy, she told herself.

She reached out and pushed him over.

The stiff body swung to the side. The hard head made a soft *clonk* as it hit the wooden arm of the chair.

Kris stared down at it, feeling strangely satisfied, as if she'd somehow taught it a lesson.

The curtains rustled against her face again. She pushed them away.

Feeling sleepy, she started back to bed.

She had only gone one step when Slappy reached up and grabbed her wrist.

About the Author

R.L. STINE is the author of more than two dozen best-selling thrillers and mysteries for young people. Recent titles for teenagers include *The Hitchhiker*, *Beach House*, and *Hit and Run*, all published by Scholastic. He is also the author of the *Fear Street* series.

When he isn't writing scary books, he is the head writer of the children's TV show *Eureeka's Castle*, seen on Nickelodeon.

Bob lives in New York City with his wife, Jane, and twelve-year-old son, Matt.

APPLE® PAPERBACKS

Exciting stories for you!